The Chronicles of Andromeda:

The Ruby of Rellene

ANNABELLA BOUK

AND

PAMELA BROOKE MCILRATH

The Ruby of Rellene

Copyright ©2016 by Pamela McIlrath and Annabella Bouk.
All rights reserved.

Cover art copyright ©2016 by Nicoletta Imbesi.
All rights reserved.

No part of this publication may be reproduced, distributed, or transmitted in any form or by any means, including photocopying, recording, or other electronic or mechanical methods except in the case of brief quotations embodied in critical reviews, articles, and certain other noncommercial uses permitted by copyright law.

This is a work of fiction. Names, characters, places, events, and incidents are either the products of the authors' imagination or used in a fictitious manner. Any resemblance to actual persons, living or dead, or actual events is purely coincidental.

ISBN-13:
978-1539619710

ISBN-10:
1539619710

DEDICATION

We would like to dedicate this book to Abby McIlrath and Robin Meeks, who have helped us improve our story telling and inspired us to keep going to be the best we can be. Thank you, Robin and Abby.

CONTENTS

Prologue	1
The Precipice of War	7
Wishing to Help	15
The Portal Room	21
Anyone Can Learn	25
Sting Arrows	29
The War Begins	33
Going to Nievia	37
Kolla	41
Arguing with Stone Walls	43
Something Shocking	47
A Broken Bridge	51
Treason	55
Pearla and Mezule	59
Old Stories	61
Sarcastic Planning	63
In Sydnia	67
Friends and Foes	71
The Ruby of Rellene	75
Ashterella	79
Myads	81

The Castle	85
Sanzwahan	87
Saved in the Nick of Time	91
The Night Beast	95
Nightmares	97
Up the Mountain	101
Sydnians	105
Myad Peak	109
Stunning	113
Last Minute	117
A Break in the Battle	121
Fen Wes	123
A Plan from the Past	125
Official	129
Lenquan Legends	133
Maybe	139
Pronunciation Guide and Maps	143

ACKNOWLEDGMENTS

We would like to acknowledge our parents, who have supported both of us in our endeavours in writing this book. Also, we would like to thank our amazing cover art artist Nicoletta Imbesi. Mrs. Kadzis, our amazing writing and grammar teacher, has made this book possible. Thank you to all of you!

Prologue

Princess Eniela's Point of View

"Ashterella," I told my youngest sister, "If you come to my room after lessons, I will tell you a story." I had just finished my lessons with Professor Sunhaye, and I was told to fetch Ashterella for hers. As we crossed the courtyard, I sighed.

I was a princess, Princess Eniela of Keedah, and was soon to be coronated Crown Princess. I had always despised turning thirteen, as I was to be coronated at the end of that year. I had *six* sisters, two older, and four younger. And in short, I had no parents.

"Alright, Eniela," Ashterella agreed. In about a minute we were at the door of the study. I waved farewell to the professor. He returned my gesture and I was on my way. Ashterella's lessons would last about two hours, so I would have time to go to the village of Shiani. I walked to the gate and as my hand touched the rusted brass latch, I heard a voice.

"Your Highness," I whirled around to find Drandin standing behind me. "May I escort you to your destination?" he asked. Drandin was the captain of the army, and was *very* chivalrous, though at times quite dull. I agreed to this, knowing he would insist if I refused, and continued on my way to the dress shop. I was hoping to have a new dress made, as my oldest sister, Chroni, made sure each one of us got a new dress for every big occasion.

"Your Highness!" the girl squeaked as I walked into the dress shop. I could tell she was a new errand-girl.

She had a countrified gown. Sanzwahanian, I guessed. Sanzwahan was a small island in the Great Ocean. I had been there last summer, and it was dreadfully hot, which explained the girl's tanned face.

"Now, now!" the shop owner reproached as she came out of the back room with an arm load of silk. "Silche, take these to Tala," she said, dumping them into Silche's arms.

"Yes, ma'am," the young girl said as she gave me a fascinated gaze. Then she turned and went off to deliver the silks.

"Oh! I beg your pardon, Your Highness!" the shopkeeper exclaimed.

"Quite alright," I said, chuckling quietly to myself as she tried not to stare at the tall man with a sword hanging from his belt. Drandin's scarlet tunic was shimmering in the light, causing a glare to come off the stunning silks, which were stacked neatly on the counter.

"What can I do for you, Your Highness?" the shop owner asked, drawing her attention away from Drandin with a *tremendous* effort.

"What? Oh, yes!" I said, "I need a new gown for my stay in Lenqua." My sisters and I were all going to Lenqua for my coronation to Crown Princess Eniela. That title seemed much too fancy for my taste.

Many people thought that the coronation should be held in Keedah, and rightfully so. However, it was Keedan custom to be coronated in a different country to show that being royalty in one country meant kindness to all. My twin sister, Genia, was to be coronated in Schipher, a country southwest of Keedah.

"Oh, yes, Your Highness!" the shopkeeper clapped her hands together joyfully, "We would be honored to work on your gown!" she paused before continuing, "May I ask what colors Your Highness wishes?"

"I was thinking pale blue with silver embroidery," I told her, imagining the gown in my head.

The small lady smiled, "That would look splendid."

"Ma'am?" Silche mumbled, as she came back from delivering silk.

"Yes, Silche?" the lady asked, annoyed.

"Duchess Seniea wants golden ribbons for her gown. Shall I go to the market and fetch some?" Silche questioned.

"Yes! Do go at once," the shopkeeper said, clearly wanting to get rid of her, "Duchess Seniea is one of our best patrons."

As Silche scurried off, the lady turned back to me. "Anything else Your Highness wishes? Cakes? Tea?" she asked, gesturing to a door. I guessed it lead to her customer parlor.

"No, thank you," I said. I had no wish to sit in a frilly parlor for several minutes. I had enough of that back at the palace. The lady gave me a smile (me or Drandin that is; I couldn't tell), which I returned before heading out the door.

When we reached the gates, I thanked Drandin for escorting me. I wandered around the palace gardens for a few minutes before beginning the maze to my room. Through the main hall, up the left set of stairs, turn right, down another set of stairs, walk through another hall, turn left, and there was my room. Quite a long walk, and as I was tired, it seemed endless.

After a long trek, I finally reached my room, I thought about the story I was going to tell Ashterella. *I will tell her of the time when the* Gloria (our royal ship) *was caught in a storm. She was only three years of age then*, I thought.

I replayed the story in my head. It was quite a dreadful storm. The rain was pounding, the thunder was booming, and the waves were splashing on the upper deck. Rain, thunder, waves… I fell asleep dreaming about the storm.

The next thing I knew, the village bell was marking the time. Three rings of the bell, that meant it was three o'clock. *Ashterella will be here in about thirty minutes*, I thought. I readied my room, which was as neat as it always was.

I plopped on my canopy bed, reconsidering the story I had chosen to tell Ashterella. I *did* have a record of changing my mind quite a lot. *Perhaps I should tell her of the time when we were captured by the Sydnians in the War for Keedah. Or I could tell her of Chroni's coronation to High Crown Princess Chroni*, I thought.

I decided to stay with the story of the *Gloria*, as she would probably like that one best. I fidgeted with my enchanted ruby necklace I always wore; I couldn't take it off even if I wanted to. No one else besides my sisters knew about the necklace, not that it was a hard secret to keep. The necklace never did anything.

Annyay, my faithful servant and friend, appeared in the doorway. "Your Highness," she said, "Professor Sunhaye has asked me to tell you that Ashterella will be a bit late."

"Thank you, Annyay," I answered.

She left and I wondered what could be keeping Ashterella. As I waited, my mind drifted off to the coming Year of Love.

Not many princesses looked forward to the Year of Love, and Genia, Leirra and I were no exception. At the end of the year, Genia and I would be coronated crown princesses. Leirra would be coronated the following year, as she was only twelve. In two years, it would be the Year of Love, and we would have to be engaged at age fifteen, and fourteen for Leirra. I tried to comfort myself by saying it was two years away, but that wasn't any help. I was thirteen, and I was supposed to be engaged in two years? I would of liked to give a slap in the face to whoever thought *that* was a good idea. My sister, Leirra, appeared in the doorway.

"Eniela?" she said, "Chroni has called a conference."

"What? Again?" I groaned, "I say, we have been having a lot of them lately!" I joined my sister and we started making our way to the council (or conference) room. Sometimes, I felt like the most unlucky princess in the entire world of Lydria. No, I felt as the most unlucky person in the whole of the Andromeda Galaxy!

Chapter 1

The Precipice of War

Princess Eniela's Point of View

"We must not be too suspicious of them!" Drandin, the captain of the army, argued. My oldest sister Chroni was going at it with Drandin again, which was the only interesting thing about conferences. We were all seated at a table, which seemed to stretch on for a mile. My six sisters and I were seated on one side, and the captains of the army, navy, and guards were on the other side, along with the captain of the archers.

"I'd rather not be surprised by an attack, thank you," Chroni shot back, finally losing her usually unbreakable self-control. My eyes flashed toward Genia, who seemed to have zoned out. I had to hold back from giggling. Then I got an idea.

"Why don't we just watch the Sydnians and the Turbotines from afar?" I asked, breaking my don't-speak-as-much as-possible rule.

"We *do* have more allies then them," Corinthia added in a barely audible whisper.

Corinthia was to be engaged in two years at age seventeen and she was courting Prince Armandi of Hacoloe, which was a large county of islands in the northwest.

Drandin was now as red as a rose, for he knew that if I spoke up, *everyone* was tired of the argument. "I apologize, Your Highness, I must be off to see the army now," he stated as he spun around on his heel and left. Chroni sighed and waved everyone out of the room, except for us. Us meant my older sister Corinthia, me, Genia, and my other younger sisters: Leirra, Senwerei, and Ashterella.

Chroni was not married or engaged. That was because she could choose whether or not to marry, since she acted as queen, though her title was High Crown Princess Chroni. She couldn't legally become queen until she was twenty-five, and that was seven years away.

As soon as everyone else was out of the room, Chroni spoke, "As you all know, two years from now is the Year of Love-"

I couldn't help it. I cut Chroni off by groaning audibly. She silenced me with a look and continued, "Corinthia is courting Prince Armandi of Hacoloe. So that means that Crown Prince James of Schipher, Crown Prince Luka of Schipher, and Crown Prince Matthew of Lenqua are going to be betrothed in the next Year of Love. Leirra will be thirteen next year, so she will be Crown Princess Leirra the last day of the year before the Year of Love." Chroni sat silent for a minute before saying, "I have asked all of them over for a score of days."

Genia, Leirra, and I all turned scarlet red at her words while Senwerei and Ashterella giggled uncontrollably. I had looked for a way out of the Year of Love, but the only way out of it was if the country was in crisis. It seemed rather selfish to put a country in to peril because I didn't want to be engaged. Unless, of course, that country was Sydnia. There were five years in between each Year of Love, and I dreaded it.

"Crown Prince James and Crown Prince Luka will arrive today, and Crown Prince Matthew next week," Chroni reported. Then she dismissed us with a wave of her hand. Genia, Leirra, and I were the first ones out of the door.

Luka and I had a "special" feeling for each other, and we often spent wonderful days in the village. Even though he was *just* a year older, we still had great times. We would go shopping for books and then stop in at the baker's shop and get some muffins. We would then walk all the way to the massive farm house, which was owned by royalty, and sit underneath the risen structure, eating our muffins. We liked to tease each other, and we both *always* had some sense of sarcasm.

Matthew was like the older brother I never had, as he was *just* two years older than me (he was exactly two years and eleven days older). He was kind, caring, and protective, but fun and adventurous. Many times we would meet each other at the archery field very early in the morning and practice. We both were perfect shooters; we rarely missed. After practicing, we would jump on our horses and follow the archery trail we made. The hardest target was a piece of wood dangling from a rope. We had to make our horses jump and shoot the target at the same time. That was no easy feat.

Prince James and I had no feelings for each other; it was more of an awkward politeness and as for Prince Armandi, I thought he was selfish and rude. I didn't even *pretend* to like him.

Drawing myself out of my thoughts, I walked briskly into my room. In my wardrobe I found all of my clothes: riding gowns, tunics and pants (which Chroni only let me wear when we were traveling to Lenqua, where that was a popular style), simple gowns, and sweaters. The ballroom gowns were kept in one of the many spare rooms.

I decided to wear my favorite gown: a blue simple gown with lace-like straps. I changed my silky black boots to tan sandals, and tied my hair with a matching ribbon. I sighed as I looked in the full length mirror. Sometimes I wished I wasn't a princess. Everything was so complicated and fancy. Someone knocked at the door. I made sure to cover the lantern in the dressing-room before I jogged over to the double door and threw it open. Ashterella bounced in, smiling.

Ashterella was ten years of age, the youngest princess. We were very close. She loved to listen to my stories about the past. Since she was only one day old when the War of Keedah began, she didn't remember it. I was only three years old, so I didn't remember much either, but the war lasted until I was eight, so I remembered some of the later events in the war.

Hacoloe, Schipher, and Lenqua had fought on our side, against the Sydnians and the Turbotines. The war started because my father, King Meyon, had been killed by the Sydnians. He had been in Sydnia to get medicine for my mother who had been sick. My mother, Queen Nereve, died giving birth to Ashterella. Ashterella managed to keep alive, but who would have been my first brother, Harbin, died with my mother. One of the last events that happened, Ashterella's favorite story, was that we got captured. We were sailing to Lenqua to keep away from the main battlefront. The ship we were on was the old royal ship: *The Golden Wind*. A Sydnian warship appeared-

"Eniela? Hello?" Ashterella snapped her fingers, trying to get my attention.

"Hmm? Oh, yes," I said, pushing the war memories to the back of my head.

"When Luka gets here, can I go to the village with you?" she asked hopefully.

"What makes you think that we are going to the village?" I avoided her question.

"You *always* go to the village," Ashterella answered.

Before I could think of a good answer, the royal trumpets sounded. I looked out my massive window and saw that the Schipherian royal ship, *The Swan*, was anchored in the harbor. Ashterella and I raced out the door without a word. We ran up some stairs, down some stairs, turned left, and we were finally in the courtyard.

All of my other sisters were already out, in a perfect line from oldest to youngest, with spaces for Ashterella and me. Just as we took our places, the royal procession came through the palace gates. Two guards, fully armed, lead the way. They stopped in front of us, and with a clap, they each stepped to one side, revealing James and Luka, both looking very princely.

I immediately blushed at the sight of Luka but tried to hide it by waving me fan as though I was hot. This, of course, was very unlikely in a place as cold as Keedah. The guards went around behind the princes. Then they bowed and returned to the harbor. I saw that the princes' luggage was placed behind them. We all burst out laughing (James scowled) Chroni tried to hold back, but she couldn't help laughing as well. The Schipherian way of doing things was very army-like. Before I knew what was happening, Luka and I were heading to the palace library.

The library had bookshelves covering two of the four walls. On one wall, sofas sat underneath a colossal window. On the remaining wall there was a door and several tables. It was an amazing place.

"Oh! Have you read Lenquan Mythology?" I asked, fingering a big book.

"We have a copy of that in our library too. I have read it once or twice," he answered.

"As usual, one step ahead of me," I laughed.

"I have more time to read than you do," He commented humbly.

"On your way to check the army?" I asked.

"Yes. Father keeps me busy doing that all year round," Luka answered.

"Things in Schipher are very army-like."

"That's one way to put it."

"Did you hear about the discovery of that other planet?" I asked my friend.

"Oh, Lorrainia?" he asked.

"Yes, that's it," I replied.

"We've already established a portal there," he said, as he pulled off a Hacoloe history book off a low shelf.

"Already?" I asked, whirling around, "We're going to have a portal ceremony tomorrow."

"We're always very quick with that sort of stuff. Has Lenqua established one yet?" he questioned as he put back the book of Hacoloe history.

"I don't think so," I answered.

After a few more minutes discussing Lorrainia and books, we made our way to the near-by village of Shiani. It was known as the Royal Village, since it was so close to the palace. Just before we reached the half-way point between the palace and the village, someone called to me.

I whirled around to see Rena, a maid of the palace, standing there. She smiled weakly, and I could tell something was wrong. "High Crown Princess Chroni wishes you both to be present at a conference immediately."

✕

As I entered the room for the second time in a day, I started to groan. However, I spotted Matthew sitting on the far right side of the table. He smiled at me, and I returned the smile. After everyone had taken a seat, Chroni stood up, frowning.

"Sydnia and Turbotia have declared war on us," she said grimly. Gasps and mutters echoed around the room. "Also, they have stated war on Lenqua and Schipher." I glanced at Matthew, who was also grave-faced.

"If I may," Matthew interjected, "I am here as a representative for my father. He has sent me here not by the traditional royal way, by boat, but by portal."

Of course, I knew that royalty only use portals in emergencies. I had seen the portal room of the palace once or twice. If Matthew's father sent him here through portal that meant Lenqua was not ready for war.

"And he has done so because Lenqua is not prepared for war. We are a country who strives for peace, so we do not have massive armies on stand-by," he stated, glancing at Luka, who gave a half-smile. Luka was almost always optimistic, which countered my half-time pessimism.

"Schipher, of course, has an army at the ready. As I have only just heard this news, I do not know what my father plans to do," James stated politely, ignoring Matthew's apparent gesture to Luka.

"The thing is," Chroni said, "Sydnia and Turbotia have a new ally."

"Who?" I asked before I could stop myself.

"Hacoloe," she answered, glancing at Corinthia, who bit her lip. From her reaction, I guessed she had already heard the news.

"Hacoloe?" I exclaimed, not caring if I sounded like a child, "But they're *our* ally!"

"Father never trusted them," Luka said, "*We* never directly allied with them." I shot a glance at my friend as if to tell him to stop it. Despite the situation, he grinned.

"This is the end of the Four Allies Alliance," Chroni reported, "with Hacoloe," she added quickly, seeing everyone's confused faces. "And is the beginning of the Tri-Alliance."

"And it's a Tri-War," I stated, and indeed it was.

Chapter 2

Wishing to Help

Princess Anelzea's Point of View

DeNell's Perch was the perfect place to go to get away from the castle. The beautiful mountainside littered with flowers felt like home unlike any other place. One day as I roamed the Perch collecting flowers, I saw something I hadn't seen in a long time. A certain flower called Tayel.

"Tayel," I murmured, shocked. Tayel was very rare, but when it *did* grow it was in large amounts. Its silver, red, and gold flowers shined in the sunlight, making the flower look even more beautiful.

I grabbed all of the tayel and put it in the pouch I always wore on my dress sash. I took one flower out and said, "Take my message to Verella Evadell, a vider: Look what I found!"

Then I let go and it drifted away. While I was waiting, I busied myself by collecting more flowers. There weren't many other flowers besides kedion, the occasional kinlil medicine flower, and the lilta flower. When I was ready for a rest, I sat down in the light green grass which covered the landscape like carpet. The fervid sun enclosed me in a warm blanket, and I struggled against sleep. After a couple minutes I heard footsteps not far away.

"Hello, Verella," I welcomed my friend, not needing to turn around.

Being a vider, Verella could jump much higher than a human could and had long grass for hair. She and I had known each other pretty much as long as I could remember. She was a descendant of Nievia, the Vider who had found our country. Nievia had chosen not to be queen, so my own ancestor, Linjia became queen. The country, however, had been named for Nievia.

"*Zelt*, Your Highness," she said.

"What's '*zelt*' again?" I asked, ignoring her false fanciness. She always teased me, because she could have easily been the princess instead me.

She rolled her eyes, "Hello."

Verella had been trying to teach me Vidish (the language of viders) for years but I never caught on. In emotional times, however, I could speak it fluently. Verella said that it was quite common.

"You know, Lydria found out about us," she said.

"Really?" I asked. The nearby planet of Lydria had been discovered by viders a few years back, but I never had any interest in it.

"Yep. And they're on the precipice of war."

"Oh, no," I gasped, "I wish we could help somehow. Though I wouldn't want to get pulled into a war." I was never fond of the idea of killing people, not that it mattered. I didn't know how to use any weapon.

"Maybe you can convince the Queen to help," she suggested.

My face became very grim, "Verella, my aunt *cannot* know about this. She would join the wrong side." My heart began pounding, as it always did when someone mentioned my aunt, the evil queen of Nievia.

"You don't think-"

"Yes, my aunt would join Sydnia." I remembered a book I had read a few months back about Lydria. We didn't know much about it, but we did know the a few of the countries and the grave and long-lasting wars that went on there.

"Then what can we do?" Verella asked, her eyes dropping to the ground as if she expected to find an answer there.

"I don't think we can do anything," I told her helplessly. It was the first time I had said that sentence.

✻

A couple days later I woke up to the sound of frog-like talking. I grinned and drew the curtains. The sunlight stared through my window, temporarily blinding me. When the effect wore off, I could see a familiar creature.

"Capels!" I exclaimed. I got dressed then ran down stairs, made a few turns, and ran out the massive door into the courtyard. The huge, red, talking frogs were floating near my window. I smiled.

"Hey! Down here!"

They flew down not-so-gracefully. The three capels steadied themselves after the landing.

"Princess Anelzea of Nievia," croaked one, "May I have the honor of taking you on a ride?"

I beamed. "Certainly!"

I climbed on to his back. As it had been many years since I had ridden a capel, it was quite a surprise to find his back dry, not slippery. He took off and began to fly through the air.
"Can we pick-up Verella?" I asked.

"Of course," he replied.

I directed him to Verella's little hut. On the way, I took in the amazing view. In the distance I could see DeNell's Perch.

"There she is!" I said, gesturing to a figure outside the brown hut.

He swooped down and grabbed her. She screamed.

"I didn't mean like that!" I laughed.

"You're going to get it for this one, Anelzea!" she shouted. I helped her up onto the capel's back, where she mocked shoving me off. I laughed.

We kept going for a while, then Verella said, "What's that?"

I looked down and saw something, but I couldn't quite make it out.

"Go closer," I commanded.

We went nearer. The capel set Verella down and alighted on the ground. What looked like a swirl of mist was standing in front of us. Its mist was blue, unlike the green mist of the portals in Lorrainia. That meant it had been made in a different world.

"A portal!" I gasped, as I hadn't seen one for a while.

Verella grinned. "Do you dare?"

"Yes I do," I replied to my friend.

We stepped into the portal side-by-side. The mist engulfed me until I couldn't see anything, even Verella. "Verella?" I called, but the mist blocked the sound. It was my first time in a portal, and I wished it would be one of my last. Finally, when we emerged, we were completely dry. We were in a room I had never seen. I looked back at the portal and took a step forward, away from it. Little did I know that I would see many things- some great and some terrible- before I saw home.

Chapter 3

The Portal Room

Princess Eniela's Point of View

We had the portal ceremony two days ago, but no one dared to go through it yet. Another world was out there, and there was no saying where that portal went. Luka and James had staked out in a guest room, talking about the consequences of war. Their room was next to mine and I could hear everything. I spent many sleepless nights thinking about their grim words. Matthew stayed as well, though he never told me why.

"What are you thinking about, Eniela?" someone said. I glanced up to see Matthew, trotting along beside me. Matthew was a great friend and a good someone to talk to.

"Just about Lorrainia," I told my friend.

"No," he told me, matter-of-factly.

"No what?" I asked him, though I was sure he knew what I was planning.

"You are not going to Lorrainia," he stated as we came to a halt in the hallway.

"What?" I said, pretending to be surprised. In reality, I was pretty flattered that Matthew knew me so well.

"Don't 'what?' me," he said, "I know you're planning to go through that portal."

I continued walking, but I turned my course to the portal room.

"Don't deny it," Matthew told me, then he realized where we were going, "No, Eniela."

"I'm not going to go through," I said, casually, "I just want to see."

"*Fine*," said Matthew, knowing I couldn't be swayed.

We rounded a corner, and a door met us halfway down the hallway. Giggling quietly, I banged on the hidden panel which held the key. I inserted the key into the hole, and twisted it. The lock didn't want to open, but after a minute or two I was able to come to terms with it. Too loudly, the door swung open and banged the wall. I stumbled backwards.

"Nice going, Eniela," I murmured to myself, as I traced the new dent in the wall.

"Eniela," Matthew whispered.

"What?" I grumbled as I stood up, and then I saw what he was talking about.

Two figures were emerging from the portal to Lorrainia. As they came out of the blue mist, I saw two girls, one about my age, and the other about Corinthia's age. The younger had brown-blonde hair and sparkling brown eyes, but the older had green hair and dark brown eyes.

It was then I realized that the elder actually had *grass* for hair. It was a stand off, Matthew and I against the strangers. Silence reigned the room for several moments, and it rang louder than the village bell. "Who are you?" I managed to stutter in Keedan.

The younger girl tilted her head, apparently not understanding me.

"Who are you?" I tried in Lenquan. When I spoke it, the girl looked up, surprised.

"I'm Verella," the grass-haired girl interjected in a friendly manner. She spoke perfect Lenquan, but she wasn't from Lenqua, that was for sure.

"I'm Anelzea," the younger said timidly.

Verella was clothed in tunic and pants, which looked sort of like they were made from massive leaves. Anelzea, as she called herself, was clad in a plain red gown trimmed with lace.

"I'm Princess Eniela of Keedah," I told them, and watched their eyebrows shoot up.

"I am Prince Matthew of Lenqua," Matthew stated fancily, as he performed an excellent bow.

Anelzea took a deep breath; I could hear it across the room. She came forward and said, "Actually, I'm *Princess* Anelzea of Nievia, which is in Lorrainia." Stunned, Matthew bowed a second time, much lower. (So low he may have just been collapsing from astonishment.) Also astounded, I curtseyed to the princess, and she did the same.

"If you're a princess, then where are you guards?" I asked curiously.

"No one knows we're here," Anelzea responded, "We found the portal out in a field and went through," she paused, "And the queen doesn't care enough about me to give me guards."

"Welcome to Keedah," I said cheerfully, ignoring her last statement.

"Thank you," Anelzea answered, smiling.

"Shall we go to my oldest sister, Chroni, and tell her of your arrival? She will be *dying* to meet you!" I said, gesturing as if to go to Chroni.

"No," the princess responded, "I, um, just want to see Keedah. Why is it named Keedah anyway?"

"We were once a really small country, but we were known for kindness to all countries. So, when the country was named, they named it Keedah, which means kindness to all, in Old Lenquan" I told her, glad to share some of my knowledge of history.

"Oh," Anelzea said, "Shall we go see Keedah?"

"Yes, of course," I responded, motioning for her and Verella to follow me.

"Eniela," Matthew whispered as he pulled me to the side, "How can we trust them? They might be spies!"

"They are not spies," I reassured my friend, though I was partly reassuring myself.

"Eniela…" he started, but I cut him off.

"Matthew, trust me. That's not going to happen," I paused for a few moments before I opened my mouth to tease him, but I thought better of it.

"Alright," Matthew said, apparently unpleased with the plan.

"Shall we be off?" I asked.

I led Anelzea and Verella out the door and into the main hall of the palace.

Chapter 4

Anyone Can Learn

Princess Anelzea's Point of View

"Can your country help at all?" asked Eniela after telling me further information about the war at hand. She neglected, however, to say anything about what countries were involved. It didn't matter. I knew it already.

"I'm afraid not. My aunt, the queen, is evil. There's no other way to put it. She would join Sydnia," I told my new friend with a frown.

Eniela didn't speak, but Matthew looked startled, "How does a *Lorrainian* know what Sydnia is?" Eniela shot him a glance, but his blue eyes were fixed firmly on me.

"We viders have been keeping an eye on you," said Verella, "You know, in case you needed aid."

"Even though you can't help us?" Matthew was obviously suspicious. Eniela stamped on her friend's foot (hard) as if to say "stop it". He pretended it didn't hurt, his watering eyes gave him away.

"Just because my country can't help doesn't mean the two of us can't help," I said.

"Can you use a sword?" Matthew asked.

"No."

"A bow?"

"No."

"Then what can you do?"

"Learn," said Eniela, who had been quiet for a while, "*Anyone* can learn. We can teach them, Matthew."

"Very well," Matthew grumbled, "Meet us at the archery field at noon."

✻

Noon came and we were already at the field. Matthew and Eniela came right on time and we got started right away. Verella was a natural and I wasn't too bad. Eniela kept telling us about times when she had been in archery competitions. I noticed that she never told about the ones she won. Which meant that she either didn't like to brag or she never won. I figured it was the former, as she didn't miss a shot, except for one, which she said got caught by the wind.

At one point I stopped and said, "In Lorrainia we have something called archens that can shoot arrows out of their eyes."

"Can *they* help us?" asked Eniela, turning to look at me.

"They work with my aunt."

"All of them?"

"Yes."

At about two o'clock, after seeing the nearby village and the palace, I said, "I think I should meet your parents." I meant, of course, the king and queen.

Eniela's face fell, making me worried that I said something wrong.

"It's just my sisters and me," she said.

"I'm sorry," I sympathized.

✳

"I have called this council because two Lorrainians happened to wander into our portal. This is Princess Anelzea of Nievia."

"And I am Verella Evadell, a vider," Verella said, shooting a what-about-me glance at Eniela.

"What's a vider?" Ashterella, who I met before the meeting, asked.

"Grass-hair, jump high," replied Verella shortly. I could tell she was little cross about being left out.

"Anyway," said Eniela, "Verella and Anelzea are here to help in the war."

"Your country can help?" asked Chroni, Eniela's eldest sister. I was amazed at how easily these people could speak many different languages. Along with Neivian, I could speak Teafic, Tipish, and Knockesh. I could speak a little Seekian too, as Lothoseeko was where mother grew up. Of course, these were all countries back on my home planet of Lorrainia.

Tip and Knock had been our allies when my grandmother was queen. I never forgot the languages that I had learned so young. But then my aunt became queen and she didn't trust Tip. When she broke off the alliance, Knock broke their alliance with her. Tip and Knock had been allies for centuries. They would not break that for Aunt Kolla. Another shock followed this one. Kolla allied with Teaf, the most evil country in all of Lorrainia.

"Evil queen," I muttered, not wanting to explain everything again.

"Your mother?"

"My aunt."

"So how can *you* help?" The question caught me off guard.

I paused for a moment and Verella spoke, "Mathew and Eniela are teaching us archery."

"And we brought means of communication," I said as I remembered finding the tayel back home.

"We did?" Verella asked, her eyebrows shooting up.

I opened my pouch. A sweet aroma filled the room. I pulled one single flower out of the pouch. It had been shoved in, but it was undamaged.

"Tayel. When you need to contact someone, this is all you have to do: Take my message to Eniela, Princess of Keedah, a human: Isn't this amazing?"

I let the flower go and it fluttered through the air closing midway. It alighted in Eniela's hand and opened. "From Anelzea, Princess of Nievia, a human: Isn't this amazing?" The flower's sweet voice made my own seem much higher than it really was. Everyone gasped and looked longingly at the flower.

"It is quite pretty," commented Ashterella. The middle of the flower was gold, and it was adorned by red and silver petals.

"Yes," I said, "Very pretty and very rare. Here is what I'll do: I will split it between Chroni, Eniela, Matthew, Verella, Luka, Drandin and I." It seemed like a lot of people but each of us ended up with ten flowers. I had met Luka, the prince of Schipher, and Drandin, the captain of the army, before the meeting. Luka seemed rather nice (and a little tired), but Drandin seemed grumpy. I didn't have to ask why. I knew he was under a lot of pressure because of the war.

"Now," I said, "about this war…

Chapter 5

Sting Arrows

Princess Eniela's Point of View

"So you don't want *kill* anyone in a war?" Drandin snarled at Anelzea, despite her position. His Keedan accent slipped in, making it sound like a mix of Lenquan and Keedan. I stifled a giggle. I had told everyone to speak in Lenquan so that Anelzea and Verella could understand, but Drandin didn't seem to care.

"It's a war, Anelzea," Matthew added.

"I want to help," protested Anelzea, "But I don't want to kill anyone."

"You have to kill to defeat," Drandin stated vehemently. He spoke in Keedan this time, so Anelzea's head cocked questioningly.

"Not necessarily," I contradicted in Lenquan for Anelzea, "I've seen something called Sting Arrows in Lenqua. They look like normal arrows, but when they hit someone, the person is stunned for about two hours."

"That would be perfect!" Anelzea agreed.

Suddenly, the doors of the room burst open. At once, everyone, including me, was on their feet, but it was only a flower. Tayel, as Anelzea called it. Everyone but Anelzea stared in awe of this phenomenon happening again. The gold, red, and silver flower floated gently down to Anelzea. Surprised, she opened her hand and the flower came to rest in it.

"From Kolla, Queen of Nievia, a human: Anelzea? Where are you?" the tayel flower said. The tayel said it in a worried tone, but I was sure that was *not* how Kolla said it.

"Are you going to tell her?" Verella asked her friend.

"I can't!" Anelzea replied. Then she said, "Take my message to Kolla, Queen of Nievia, a human: I am out exploring the Floating Sea." She let go of the stunning flower, and it floated out of the door. "It probably took that two days to get here."

"Maybe you should go back," Matthew suggested, again implying that he did not trust her. I gave the look to Matthew, who half-smiled sheepishly.

"No, not there, not with…" she responded, shaking her head.

"Then?" Drandin asked.

"I can help spy on Sydnia to see what they're up to," Anelzea replied simply, I noticed that she didn't show much emotion, very different from me.

"Like you've been spying on us," Matthew muttered quietly. I could barely hear him, and he was sitting on my left. He clearly distrusted the princess, and I guess he had a right. No one knew anything about her.

"No," Drandin said, "Spying is not safe. We've lost a good many spies through the years."

And he was right, we did lose many great men who were spying on Sydnia and Turbotia. After about an hour's worth of discussion, we decided to wait until the Sydnians attacked, and then have Schipher and Lenqua come and surround them. This was a tactic that Drandin had pulled out from the War of Keedah. This had been before he became Captain of the Army, and I could tell he wanted to use it for himself. I never had questioned why he was around the palace so much if he was the captain.

"I think we should go spy on Sydnia," Anelzea whispered to me as soon as my bedroom door closed. I could see that she was very stubborn.

"Alright," I agreed, as if was no big deal. "When?"

"Tomorrow."

"*Tomorrow?*"

"Yes."

Well, it would be an adventure, but at that moment, I didn't know how *much* of an adventure. Anelzea and I prepared until the moons were high in the sky. When we were both exhausted, I showed my friend to one of the many guest rooms. I helped her get settled. Ashterella had shown Verella to a guest room earlier, so almost all of the rooms were full. A lot of people were staying at one time. Even more then when we held the feast to celebrate just after Ashterella was born. But no one had been ready to celebrate yet, as it had been just after my parents died.

"Gutcha nalam," I said.

"What?" Anelzea asked, not recognizing what I had said.

"Good night," I repeated in Lenquan.

Chapter 6

The War Begins

Princess Anelzea's Point of View

"Are you sure about this?" asked Eniela as we sneaked out of the palace grounds. In the light of the moons, I could my friend was worried. I glanced back at the outline of the palace fading in the night before answering.

"Quite," I said, "But Verella will be very mad that we're going without her."

"I agree," said a voice behind us. It was, of course, Verella and I had never seen her angrier. "I'm you elder by two years," she said, "and you will not be going anywhere without me."

"Well, *I* am your superior and I will go where I please, than you very much." I said, happy to have a comeback.

"My ancestor found Nievia and if she hadn't made the mistake of letting Linjia rule, I would be *your* superior." In the light of two moons, I could see her face, crimson with anger.

"Fine," I said, "If you want to come with us you can." I didn't admit it for a long time but I was quite relieved that she was coming.

✕

We had been walking for hours and the sun was peaking above the trees.

"Matthew is going to suspect me more than ever, you know," I said.

"I've been thinking the same thing," said Eniela, "You won't gain trust by sneaking around and disobedience, as Chroni says." She said this in a mocking voice. I laughed.

"Do you sneak around often?"

Before she could answer, I heard a shout, "Where do you think you're going?"

"It's Matthew!" I murmured, trying to keep calm.

"What were you thinking?" he asked in a fury. Eniela began trying to calm the angry prince down.

But I wasn't looking at him anymore. I was looking at the group of riders coming towards us.

"Sydnians," whispered Eniela, also turning around.

"But we're not armed," I cried.

But to my surprise, Matthew had provided three bows and three quivers full of sting arrows. Later, he told me that he was going to do some scouting, and had brought along extra bows, though I suspected this was an excuse to cover up the fact that he snuck out to find the girls who snuck out.

"How did you get sting arrows?" I asked.

"Never mind that," Matthew said, "Fight!"

※

The battle had gone on for ages. Matthew used tayel to send for aid. Verella jumped to a high perch and was shooting from there. Eniela and I hid behind a hill and fired. Matthew chose a sword over a bow and was using it brilliantly. The sword gleamed as it clashed and clanged with the swords of the Sydnians. Matthew was a very good swordfighter, reminding me of one of my friends, who happened to be Prince Litey of Tip.

Suddenly, I noticed someone coming up behind Matthew. I could never have stunned the attacker with the huge crowd in the way. Without thinking, I grabbed a sting arrow and stole out from behind the small hill. The prince was fighting with a well-trained swordsman, so he had no idea of the attacker coming from behind. Ignoring Eniela's screams to go back to the hill, (she obviously didn't see the attacker) I crept up to the stealthy soldier. Just as he was raising his sword, I managed to jab the sting arrow into his back. Seconds later, Matthew managed to defeat his rival and turned to see the stunned Sydnian.

The Prince's tunic was smeared with dirt and a little bit of blood. Silently, he thanked me, and I knew at that moment I had his trust at last. I made my way back to the hill, and arrived with only a small scrape and a bruise from a tree branch that I had not seen in my hurry. With more and more Keedan forces arriving, the Sydnians hastily retreated.

The Tri-War had begun.

※

Three days after the battle, I was at dinner when another tayel flower came to me. "From Kolla, Queen of Nievia, a human: Come home now." I shoved the flower into my pouch.

"Maybe you should do it," said Chroni.

"No," I said, "I will not listen to an evil queen."

This comment was followed by a loud silence.

Chroni spoke, "Perhaps everyone should get to bed. It has been a long day."

"And there will be many long days to come, no doubt," said Eniela.

"Yes," I said grimly, "We won that battle, but this war is far from over."

Chapter 7

Going to Nievia

Princess Eniela's Point of View

It had been four days since the battle, and Anelzea insisted on staying. Matthew had stopped his complaints about Anelzea and Verella, but he still had *plenty* to say about us trying to sneak off. I knew that he was very protective of me, and I was grateful, but I really didn't know why. *Maybe he's just stressed because of the war*, I thought.

Anelzea and I kept our sting arrows and our bows on hand all the time. I really didn't mind using regular arrows, but sting arrows worked fine. The guards around the palace had been doubled in number, and it was impossible to go anywhere without seeing a guard. The Sydnians suffered a great defeat in that battle, which came to be known as The Battle of Delon, since that is where it took place.

When Anelzea saved Matthew's life, I had refused to be shown up by the newcomer. I ran into the battle, and received several cuts and bruises. When I ran out of sting arrows to throw, I gave several Sydnians black eyes by slamming them with my bow.

A Schipherian warship left harbor the day before, and it was on its way to Hacoloe. Lenqua was desperately trying to grow its army. Messages from Kolla continued to arrive. It was about a fortnight since the battle when I convinced Anelzea to go home, and to take me with her.

"Fine. I'll go home, and you do make a point," Anelzea said, "I need to hide that portal."

"Yes, and I'm coming too," I replied firmly.

"No, Eniela, You don't want to go there."

"You don't know what I want!" I was beginning to get impatient.

"But it's not safe," she protested.

"Why?"

"Because my aunt will ask how you got there!"

"She doesn't have to know I'm from Lydria."

"Very well."

Then we both went separate ways and stayed away from each other as much as possible to avoid suspicion.

It was about midday, and Anelzea and I managed to slip down to the portal room without anyone noticing. Once again, I fought with the lock on the door, and once again the door banged on the wall, making the remaining dent even deeper. I was glad that the portal room was far from any bedrooms. As Anelzea held the door open, I put the key back. Then we were ready to go.

I had never been in a portal before, and I was sort of glad about that. As soon as we stepped into the blue mist, the room began to swirl around me and mist clouded my vision. Anelzea, who had done this before, didn't seem too bothered. The mist began to layer, so much so that I couldn't even see Anelzea. A wind seemed to blow me back, and then we were there. This all must have happened in a few moments, though it seemed quite slow.

I stepped out of the mist into a beautiful field full of grass and flowers. The sun shinned as bright as it did in Sanzwahan, but it was not quite as hot. Trees danced to the tune of the wind and a river could be heard, though it was far away.

"Welcome to Nievia. We won't be here long," Anelzea said, spreading her hands out to feel the warm sun instead of the cold air of Keedah.

"Why didn't you want to come back here?" I asked, "It's beautiful!"

"Well, you know…" Anelzea trailed off, but I caught her meaning. Her aunt.

When she said that her aunt was an evil queen, I thought she was exaggerating. But now it didn't seem that way.

"Come on!" Anelzea called, "The palace is this way!"

"Wait! What about Verella?"

"She probably doesn't care."

"Well, alright." I gave in.

"Let's go!" Anelzea said as she took my hand and basically pulled me towards the palace.

On the way, I tried to teach Anelzea some Keedan, but she didn't seem to get it except for a few words. That was fine, I'd just make sure the others spoke Lenquan, which she said was also Neivian

Chapter 8

Kolla

Princess Anelzea's Point of View

As we walked through the forest in Nievia, I started telling Eniela about capels. Every time I heard a noise I began to finger my sting arrows. (I had picked them up after the battle, as they are hard to come by.) As we approached the castle, we took off our bows and quivers and hid them in the bushes. We entered the palace and into the throne room. My aunt was sitting on the throne, proud as a peacock. She was an extremely short woman with surprisingly kind-looking features. Her voice (not to mention her personality) told a different story.

"Anelzea, why did you not come back as soon as I bade you?"

"We were in a storm," Eniela lied, covering up my silence.

"And who are you?" Kolla asked in her cold, icy voice.

"Natlin," she said in careful Neivian, "I met Her Highness on the boat." Later, Eniela told me that Natlin was a character in her favorite legend.

"I see," Kolla said, obviously unconvinced, "I've called you home because I have a, well, errand for you in Teaf. Give the king my message and refuse to leave until they've agreed. I've run out of tayel."

I gripped my pouch knowing that she would go to extreme heights for the flower. She took no notice of my sudden action. She held out a letter, and I took it. We walked outside and grabbed our bows and quivers from the bushes. Then we ran.

※

When we got back to the portal, I put some tree branches around it to hide it. We went in and sprinted to Eniela's room. I tore open the letter and read it aloud:

> *To the Noble King Hantec of Teaf:*
>
> *I have received word from a certain vider that Sydnia in Lydria is at war. I have been thinking on it for many days and have decided to join them* (here Eniela gasped) *and I request that you join them as well. I do believe that by helping them we ourselves will gain power in Lydria. With us on the side of the Sydnians, Keedah and their allies will not stand a chance. And do not forget the consequences I can inflict upon you should you decline.*
>
> *Singed,*
>
> *Queen Kolla of Nievia*

I finished.

"*Sheshoc le de arion la eva!*" Eniela exclaimed, I guessed it was the Keedan language.

"What?"

"Your aunt's joining Sydnia! She *is* evil!" she repeated with just as much horror in her voice.

Chapter 9

Arguing with Stone Walls
Princess Eniela's Point of View

I couldn't believe that Kolla was joining Sydnia! For a split second, I thought that Anelzea might be a spy or might betray us, but I quickly pushed the thought aside. There was no proof, and was most likely not true at all.

"Let's tear it into tiny pieces!" I suggested.

"Do you think that will help? If Kolla comes... She's right, Eniela. With her on their side, we won't stand a chance."

"Well, if you're such a coward, maybe you're not cut out for this," I snapped, not caring if my Keedan accent slipped in.

Her face turned red and I knew I'd said something wrong.

"Anelzea, I-"

"Do you really think I'm a coward? Was I coward when I risked my life to save Matthew's?"

"Anelzea, I didn't mean it."

I was trying to apologize, but she wouldn't have it.

"You sure sounded like you meant it. And if you think I'm not cut out for this maybe I *should* leave."

"We need you here!" I cried desperately, "We need all the help we can get."

"What caused you to change your mind?" she said sarcastically, "Last time I checked you wanted me to leave," she paused for a minute, "I'm sorry. Sometimes I get upset and say things I don't mean."

"I forgive you," I said, relieved that she wasn't leaving, "I'm sorry too."

Chroni had tried everything to get me to be less stubborn, but to no avail. I was very stubborn, and *almost* proud of it.

"I forgive you. We must be the most stubborn people in Andromeda. We could argue with stone walls!"

I laughed, "I think we *are* stone walls. As stubborn as them I mean," I added hastily, noticing her confused look.

There was a sharp knock on the door. I jumped.

"Come in!"

Matthew walked in, a worried expression on his face.

"What shananagance is going on in here?" he asked, smiling kindly.

"Nothing…" I teased, grinning.

"What's that?" he questioned, referring to the note from Kolla.

"Um, nothing," I said as I shoved it under my pillow.

Anelzea grinned sheepishly.

"Eniela, I just wanted to tell you, well, stay safe!" Matthew exclaimed.

"Alright, but why are you so worried for *me*?"

"Just…" he paused, "Stay safe."

"I will."

After he left I said to Anelzea, "Next time hide the letter before someone comes in."

"Well, I didn't see you hiding it!"

"Sorry," I said. I was not going through *that* again.

Chapter 10

Something Shocking

Princess Anelzea's Point of View

We were sitting in Eniela's room on a sunny morning when a scream echoed through the palace. We both bolted to where the scream had come from. Chroni stood there, shaking, and I had never seen anyone look so scared.

"Sydnians," she said barely able to form the words, "They took Genia."

"No!" gasped Corinthia, who had also rushed to the spot of the scream.

I looked over at Eniela. She seemed to be in shock. Tears slipped from her eyes, but she made no other move.

※

Days passed, but the shock of Genia's capture did not. Corinthia was often caught pacing and whispering to herself. Chroni repeatedly snapped at people and then apologized in tears. ("The only new thing is the fact that she's apologizing," Eniela said). But Senwerei was taking it the worst. She and Genia had been very close.

"Drandin," I said, "We need to make a search party," I paused, "Now." I was not going to sit around doing nothing while Genia was suffering. He groaned. "Council," he muttered, and I was surprised that anyone else could hear him.

At the council Drandin started, "Princess Anelzea of Nievia has brought up the point that something needs to be done concerning Genia's capture. So, for anyone who wishes to join a search party, now is your opportunity."

My hand shot up, accompanied by Eniela's and Verella's. "We'll join," Verella and I said at the same time. "I'll join," Eniela echoed.

"Well," Matthew said, "I'll go."

"Luka, do you want to come?"

"I'm in!" the Schipherian prince agreed, though I'm pretty sure he muttered, "um," a few moments before. Luka had stayed here longer than his brother James to help with creating a defense for the southern border, where Keedah met Sydnia.

"Chroni, can I go?" Ashterella asked, eagerly.

"I'm not happy that Eniela is going, do you think I will let *you* go?" her oldest sister questioned.

"Well," the youngest princess of Keedah said, "I'm going to go whether you want me to or not."

"Fine," Chroni answered, giving a slight glare, "But only because I know that you would."

"I will go, of course," Drandin said.

"I'll come," a man, who looked quite a lot like Drandin, offered.

"Who's he?" I asked Eniela, who was sitting next to me.

"Thrinian," she answered in a half-whisper, "He's the head of the archers." She paused for a moment before adding, "And one of Drandin's brothers."

"How many does he have?"

"Three," she answered, "Thrinian, Trett, and Rae…" she stopped herself, "and The Great Warrior." I didn't bother to ask about her hesitation. I did, however, want to ask about The Great Warrior. It seemed like Keedans liked to do things and name things simply. Then, I couldn't help asking if they we're all as dull as Drandin.

"Thrinian is even more dull, but the others are fine," Eniela told me, "Though Thrinian *did* teach me to use a bow."

※

We set off a week later. I had managed to shove ten sting arrows in my quiver. Matthew took his sword, and Luka chose some type of short sword. Ashterella had proved to be a natural with a crossbow. Verella, Eniela, Thrinian, and I all used bows. Drandin took all the bows, arrows, and swords he could carry. I couldn't help asking if the rest of the army was still armed. He just glared at me in reply.

When we had everything, we set off, heading south towards Sydnia. I was very nervous, never having been on an adventure like this before, but I didn't show it. As we went, I constantly fingered my sting arrows. I knew danger was coming, but I had no idea of the amount of danger that would really come.

Chapter 11

A Broken Bridge

Princess Eniela's Point of View

We had set off from the palace three days ago, and we were making good progress south. I knew that the next day we would reach The Golden River, which basically split the country in half. We went by carriage. Thrinian and Matthew drove the carriage, which was drawn by two horses. Anelzea, Ashterella, Verella, and I sat in the carriage, while Luka and Drandin rode horses beside. We rode day and night. We had to go fast.

Anelzea constantly complained about being cooped up all day, but I was sort of used to it. Ashterella simply looked at the map of the world. "Once we cross the Bridge of Gold (which wasn't actually gold) over the Golden River," Ashterella stated, "We won't be far from the 'Cross River, which goes across the border. And we won't be far from Brookston!"

"What's Brookston?" Verella asked curiously.

"A big city by the rivers. It would be the capital if it wasn't so close to the border," Ashterella answered. "Anyway, we won't be far from the 'Cross River," she repeated.

"You're right," I agreed, trying to remember the information about the 'Cross River that Professor Sunhaye taught me. "But how does that help us?"

"The river will most likely be busy, will it not?" Anelzea asked.

"Certainly not," I said, recalling that Sydnians don't settle by the rivers for fear of flooding. For such bold leaders, the people seemed sort of cowardly.

"Maybe we could go that way," Ashterella suggested.

"While we're waiting we can play games," I said, bored of just talking.

So we taught Anelzea and Verella our favorite games. Yolz Yolin and Mangi Yayu involved sticks. Knotenpul and Corsta were string games. Gescha was a musical guessing game. That was Anelzea's favorite. I was very fond of Yolz Yolin and Corsta. Occasionally, Matthew and Luka would shout guesses in Gescha. Everyone could hear everyone else no matter where we were. At one point Drandin shouted a guess. We burst out laughing.

"What?" he asked, "Can't I participate in games from my childhood?"

We laughed harder. It was difficult to think that Drandin had once been a child.

When we got bored of the games, Ashterella and I took turns reciting the epic poems of Lydrian history. I also taught Anelzea and Verella a bit about Keedan culture.

"The Year of the Wind is amazing," I was telling my new friends, "One day, all the countries sail ships to the center of the planet. Then-"

The carriage jerked to a stop, throwing us all forward and cutting me off. A sharp knock shook the small door. Almost groaning, I got up and opened it. It was Matthew, grinning broadly. "We're at the Golden River," he told us, offering a hand to help us out of the carriage.

"Finally!" a happy Anelzea said.

"Excuse me, Your Highness?" Thrinian asked as he appeared from behind the carriage, "Would you mind lending me a few tayel flowers to send messages back to High Princess Chroni?"

"Of course," Anelzea said as she dug her hand into a pouch and produced five tayel.

"Thank you," he said as he took them.

"I'm afraid I have some bad news," Luka stated.

"What?" I asked, turning to see my friend who had come from the direction of the bridge.

"The bridge is broken," he answered, digging his hands into his pockets. I looked at the old, wooden bridge, which now lay in pieces. The top of the bridge was broken off, and I wondered how far along the river it was.

"What do we do now?" Anelzea asked, giving Luka a look as though it was his fault.

Luka shrugged. "I don't think there are any parts of the river shallow enough for the wagon."

"It's a deep river," I commented.

"There is a part shallow enough for the wagon," Ashterella told us, "But it's about a day's journey east."

"We don't have that time," I said helplessly.

"We could abandon the wagon and buy a new one on the other side," Matthew suggested.

"With all the people," Luka said, "without the wagon it would be chaos. Even for a few days."

I sighed helplessly, my gaze leaving my friends to the river. "Besides," I added, "we can't swim to the other side anyway."

Matthew, Luka, and Ashterella shook their heads in agreement, but Anelzea was confused. "Why not?" she asked.

"You know how cold it is here?"

"Much colder than Nievia," Anelzea replied.

"Well, the water has been in this air for many, many years," I told her, "So, it's freezing."

"Oh," Anelzea said, "I didn't think of that."

"We'd all catch e*icebe*," Luka annexed.

"What's that?" Verella questioned.

"It's what you can get if you are in freezing water for too long," Matthew responded for me.

"We'd better set up camp here for the night," Ashterella suggested.

Chapter 12

Treason

Princess Anelzea's Point of View

Morning passed and we still had no idea how to cross the river. I was amazed at how the sun caught the waves, making it seems as if many lights were flashing under the water. Whoever named it The Golden River had named it perfectly. I left my bow and quiver in the wagon so that I could stretch.

As I played with Ashterella (we were playing Yolz Yolin) I suddenly found a bow pointing right at me. Out of the corner of my eyes, I could tell the arrow was not a sting arrow. It was a regular arrow. Without thinking about it, I grabbed a nearby rock and threw it at the bow, breaking it. Then I looked at the owner and gasped. I watched as the figure of none other than Thrinian disappeared into the nearby woods. I got my bow and quiver from the wagon, worrying that Sydnians were close.

※

"It's the only way!" I insisted.

"We *can't* abandon the wagon," Luka said, rather forcefully, "What about the horses?" His Schipherian accent slipped in, making me bite my lip at the odd sounding sentence.

"*Horses* can swim. *Wagons* can't"

"Very well, have it your way," he said, slowly realizing that I was *never* worth ever putting up a fight with.

"But it's freezing," Verella argued.

"It will make us go across quicker," I replied. My vider friend shrugged as if to say "don't say I didn't tell you."

We untied the horses from the wagon and wadded across. The water went up to my thighs. Eniela was right, it was freezing. The cold air of Keedah must have affected it over the many years. All of a sudden, it struck me that Matthew hadn't said a word since Thrinian's betrayal.

"Matthew, are you all right?" I asked, shivering.

"He knew all our plans!"

I had been secretly worried about that also. Then, I realized Eniela hadn't said much either since I told her of Thrinian.

"Eniela, what's wrong?"

"Thrinian," she answered. "I just don't believe it. He's the one who taught me to use a bow…"

"I don't think any of us *want* to believe it," I told her.

Verella hopped up onto the rocky shore and helped the rest of us up. Though the air was cold, the sun quickly dried us. It was only a few minutes before I spotted something in the distance. As we came closer, I saw it was a city of ruins.

"What happened?" Verella asked.

"This is the Kurah Ruins," Eniela replied, "It was burned by the Sydnians in the War of Keedah. Fortunately, everyone got out."

"How?" I inquired.

"They smelled smoke and ran."

"That's good."

"Why did they burn it?" Verella inquired.

"We had a store of weapons hidden in the city, and the Sydnians found it."

"It was once a beautiful city. Some called it Enda." Luka added.

I recognized the Keedan word for beauty. Only the foundations of houses and stores remained. A few stone towers remained, but they were scared by the fire. I could imagine once amazing gardens and buildings. Eniela teared up, no doubt mourning for the lost city. In particular, a ruined bell tower caught my eye. Vines were growing, and it was overrun with moss. The stone was black, scorched by the flames of long ago. It was at that moment I was beginning to understand just how horrible the Sydnians were.

I thought of Nievia. The villages and cities that had once been beautiful were heartbreaking to enter. People hardly got enough to eat. Everyone lived in small huts. I had visited these villages when my grandmother was queen and they were amazing. But then Kolla became queen. And she wanted everything for herself.

I noticed at that moment that everyone was staring at something. Following their gaze, I saw a portal. And my parents stood in front of it.

Chapter 13

Pearla and Mezule

Princess Eniela's Point of View

A woman and a man stood before us, blocking the portal. Matthew, who was next to me, grabbed my hand. Luka's hand slithered to his short sword. Ashterella squealed, and Anelzea stood motionless staring at the people. It was hard to read her face, but it seemed like she knew the people.

"Anelzea?" the woman asked, relaxing her hold on her bow.

I, however, gripped my bow tight. *Who are these people*, I thought.

Before Anelzea could answer, Luka stepped in front of her, "That depends. Who are you?"

Anelzea shoved Luka away, and stepped past. "Mother? Father?" she asked.

"Anelzea!" the woman exclaimed as she rushed forward and embraced Anelzea. The man followed her, and embraced his daughter too.

My heart burned at the sight of a girl my age hugging her parents.

That should be me hugging my parents, I thought jealously.

Matthew, guessing my emotions, gave my hand a little squeeze. I gave him a half-smile. Luka smiled sadly. I then remembered that his mother had died a few years back during a trip to Sanzwahan. I gave him a empathizing smile.

A tear slipped down my cheek.

※

"So you're Anelzea's parents?" I asked for the third time.

We were sitting on the grassy bank on the other side of the Golden River. I couldn't believe these people were actually Anelzea's parents. I envied her, at least she *had* parents. Mine were both dead, *and* my sister was in danger.

"Yes," Anelzea's mother, Pearla, replied simply. She was patient with my curiosity, which was the complete opposite of Chroni's *impatience*.

"Have you been apart for a long time?"

"No, just since she came here," Mezule (Anelzea's father) said.

"But it *seemed* like a long time." Anelzea added.

This remark made me angry. *If you think that is a long time try living without them for ten years.* But I didn't say anything aloud. Either I was too choked up or too mad, but it didn't matter. Anelzea was my friend, and I had to be happy for her.

"How did you know Anelzea was here?" Matthew questioned.

"Yes, tell us," echoed Luka, who was enjoying the company of Anelzea's parents quite a bit.

Chapter 14

Old Stories

Princess Anelzea's Point of View

"Well, if by *here* you mean this river, it was luck. If you mean Lydria, I have been in touch with Verella," Mother said. I shot a glance to Verella, who smiled sheepishly.

"We will certainly be joining you in your search," said Father.

"Thank you," said Luka, "We are in need of the help."

※

"So what you're saying is that your parents ought to be the king and queen, but your father's younger sister stole the throne?"

"Yes."

"Why did he allow it?" Eniela was utterly bewildered.

I didn't understand Eniela sometimes. I tried to remember her tragic past, but I was more focused on my parents. "No one dared to stand up to Kolla. You should understand. You heard her: 'Don't come back until they agree!' Or something like that anyway." I grinned bashfully.

Eniela was fidgeting with a menikat fruit. She had told me that the small, round, orange fruit was grown in many orchards all over Keedah. She didn't care much for them, but that is all the food we packed, except for a little bread. I rather liked the sour fruit; it looked like regoria, a fruit which was rare back home. However, regoria was sweet.

"We ought to be going," said Ashterella, interrupting our conversation. She held up her map, "We have a long way to go."

Nobody bothered to argue, even me.

The there were four horses and nine of us (not to mention two tents, a bundle of food, and a lot of swords, bows, and arrows, which made a problem. Finally, we arranged for Eniela, Ashterella, Verella, and I to ride the horses which would also carry some cargo.

I mounted the brown horse, who seemed to be rather lax. I hadn't ridden in a while, so it took a little bit to get used to being on the back of a horse again. Eniela, who was very happy she had a riding dress, was seated quite comfortably. As there were only two saddles, I had one and Verella had the other.

Ridding sidesaddle was not easy, as you have to turn your head to look where you were going. Eniela and Ashterella, however, were riding bareback, which meant they had no saddles. I couldn't imagine how much that had to hurt, but they didn't seem bothered.

Chapter 15

Sarcastic Planning

Princess Eniela's Point of View

The border of Sydnia became closer and closer each minute. Matthew and Luka were very quiet, causing tension to rise up between everyone. Anelzea and her parents chatted away while the rest of us trotted along in silence.

"How are we going to find Genia?" Luka asked two days before we were to reach the border. His brown eyes were filled with sympathy and worry.

"Easy. We'll go to where they keep important prisoners," I said, sounding much more confidant than I really was.

"Where is that?"

"We'll ask."

"Oh yes, we can do that," the prince said sarcastically, "as long as we don't mind being put there ourselves."

"Oh," I said, "I hadn't thought of that."

"Any ideas?" he asked.

"What are you talking about?" Anelzea inquired, walking up to us. She always seemed to want to know everything that was going on.

"Trying to figure out how to avoid being recognized," I answered.

"Do you have any ideas, Anelzea?" Luka asked.

"No," she said after thinking for a moment. "None at all."

I started thinking about when I had been captured in the War of Keedah. We had been led there blindfolded so I couldn't figure out where it was from that experience. Then Luka's words came back to me. *As long as we don't mind being put there ourselves.* All at once a plan hatched in my mind.

"The window!" I said.

"What is it?" Anelzea and Luka asked at the same time.

"Well," I replied, "I *do* remember a little about the important prisoner cell," I paused, "One and a half stories up there's a window."

"How does that help us?" Luka questioned.

"It doesn't have bars and the ledge is big enough for multiple people to stand on. Verella could jump up to it and use a rope to help the rest of us up."

The two looked at me like I was daft.

"How are we supposed to get the rope in without being caught?" Anelzea asked.

"I'm the Princess of Keedah and the Queen of Hiding Things. Trust me," I said with a grin.

"Wouldn't they think it was a trick if we just went walking through the streets of Sydnia?" Anelzea asked.

"Probably," I admitted, "No matter how much I hate to say it, the Sydnians are smart."

"Perhaps we could pretend like we were trying to sneak through," Luka suggested.

"I doubt that will work," Anelzea argued.

"Do you have any other ideas?" I snapped. "I'm sorry," I quickly said. "I'm just-"

"It's alright," Anelzea replied.

"Anyway, anyway, anyway," I said, shooting a glance at Luka, "We've got to figure out a plan."

"That's the best and only plan we have."

"Well," I said thoughtfully, "we'll have to plan the details."

Chapter 16

In Sydnia

Princess Anelzea's Point of View

The plan was simple: walk out into the streets. People knew who we were, which made the plan easy. Matthew walked to my left, Eniela to my right, and Luka walked on her right. The rest of the group walked behind us, including Ashterella.

Sydnian people started whispering and pointing at us, but we kept going. We all started a conversation in Keedan, to draw more attention. I struggled to keep up with the rapid Keedan but added in, best I could (Nievia spoke the same as Lenqua, Tip and Knock as Schipher, Teaf as Sydnia, and Nellic as Keedah. Kolla never got along with the Nelicee royalty so I didn't pick up on the language well.) We were, from what I could understand, talking about the capture of Genia. A small group of soldiers appeared out of nowhere.

"You all! Lay down your weapons now!" one of them yelled. I groaned. We had completely forgotten about our weapons. Now we were losing them to the Sydnians. Luckily, Drandin, who had waited back out our camp, had some weapons. They took our weapons and forced us to give up our tayel. It amused me to think of what they would try to do with it. However, I managed to hide my pouch. I would not lose it.

We all dropped our weapons to the ground, except Eniela. She didn't bring her bow with her for some reason. "What tricks are you up to, girly?" A soldier asked her.

"I don't have any weapons," she replied in perfect Sydnian.

"Don't try to fool me," the soldier said, "I heard you speaking that pretty little traitor language of Keedan a minute ago, Princess. Now, reveal your weapon!"

"I don't have any weapons," Eniela repeated.

The soldier gave up, and signaled to the other soldiers to lead us to the prison, blindfolded. I wondered what Eniela's angle was. She didn't have her bow, or a sword, or anything. Did she even have an angle? It didn't even matter, we weren't staying long anyway.

As we were being led to the cell, she whispered to me, "I have a dagger in my boot."

Wondering how she thought of that trick, I realized it was probably something Drandin or Luka taught her. I smiled slightly, as the rope was nowhere to be seen. Eniela was right, she was the queen of hiding things.

The plan was working great. As the soldiers led us to the cell, I tried not to grin and blow it. Suddenly, the soldiers started whispering. I groaned. They knew. I could hear them leading Verella to a different place and us to the highly-guarded cell. When we entered the cell Genia ran to us. Eniela said something in rapid Sydnian to the soldiers, but I'm not certain what she said. I know it wasn't nice at *all*.

"What happened and who are they?" she asked in Keedan, motioning to Mother and Father. I could understand her well enough. So could Mother and Father. Eniela went on to explain everything that had happened since Genia had been captured.

"What about you?" she asked, "How were you captured?"

"Thrinian," she replied gravely, "He said he was going to help me practice archery. When we got to the field, there were a lot of Sydnians. I was helpless. When I was being dragged off, I caught a glimpse of Chroni. I wanted to tell her about Thrinian's treachery, but if I drew attention to her, they would capture her too. Then she screamed. I thought they would find her, but they didn't hear."

We defiantly heard, I thought.

"So how are we going to get out?" asked Luka, "We have seven people that we have to get out of this cell."

"What about me?" asked a low misty voice. A girl about my age stepped out of a shadowy area. "Please get me out too."

Chapter 17

Friends and Foes

Princess Eniela's Point of View

"Who are you?" Anelzea asked, voicing what I was thinking. The girl's hair framed her pale face, reminding me a little bit of Ashterella's frightened face when the *Gloria* was caught in a storm. Her dark brown hair framed her dark blue eyes, and her pale face seemed as white as the palace walls back home.

"My name's Amayda," she answered, slowly. She spoke Sydnian so I figured she'd been here for a while. "Who are *you*?"

"I, uh…" I said, not sure if I should tell the stranger.

"She knows who I am," Genia whispered.

"I'm Princess Eniela of Keedah," I told her, reassured. I spoke in Sydnian and hated every word.

"I'm Princess Anelzea of Nievia."

"I'm Prince Luka of Schipher," Luka said, purposefully leaving out the 'Crown' part out.

"I am Crown Prince Matthew of Lenqua."

"Why are you-"

"Well, well, well!" a voice said, cutting me off. We all whirled around the face the front of the cell, where someone *all* too familiar stood.

"Fen Wes," I growled, naming the Sydnian general.

"I must be quite popular for you to know who I am, princess," he said with a smirk. His black hair blended in with his mostly-black clothes, and his eyes were smiling with pride.

"I've heard your name enough with the way you help meddle with my family," I answered. "What are *you* doing here?"

"I heard you were in town," he said, mockingly, "And I thought I would pay you a visit."

"Thank you for accepting our invitation," my reply came sharp and sarcastically.

Fen Wes' gaze flickered to Anelzea, and landed on Luka with a chilling glare. "Well, well, well, if it isn't my old friend," he said, his voice dripping with sarcasm.

"Well, well, well, well, well, well," I repeated, taunting the general.

His cold glare turned to me for a second before going back to Luka. However, Fen Wes' eyes stopped for a moment on someone behind me. A bit of interest sparked in his eyes and was that kindness? No, I was seeing things. A shiver crawled up my spine.

"Fen Wes," Luka spoke, his voice hinting a little bit of fear, "Long time, no see." Luka was the master at sarcasm.

"Yes, it has been a long time," Fen Wes replied with a snarl.

That doesn't mean I've forgotten!" said Luka angrily.

Fen Wes laughed. "I wouldn't expect you to. But it wouldn't have happened if you had gone alone. *You* brought him into the danger."

"I didn't want to. My father made me bring him. It's you who brings others into danger."

"Think what you want, but it *was* your fault."

"Don't listen to him Luka; he's trying to weaken you!" I told him softly. I couldn't remember exactly what Fen Wes was talking about, but I tried to comfort my friend all the same.

"I might be," Fen Wes said, "I just can't wait to finish what I started. It *is* nice to see old friends again." This last sentence was so angering, I could not hold my tongue any longer.

"None of us are in a good mood today, are we?" I interjected before any more words could be spoken.

"Your little plan has failed," Fen Wes said, (as if we didn't know that already) "and now the King himself is going to pay a visit."

"What plan?" Anelzea asked with false innocence.

"You brought along a vider," he said, "We have one here in Sydnia too."

I saw Amayda's hands form fists. Anelzea eyes widen in surprise. All of the voices seemed to echo, while Genia and I looked to each other. The King Ciscisus of Sydnia was coming *here*. He was known to show no mercy, especially to any Keedan prisoners. *He* was the one who ordered my father to be killed.

"Eniela?" Matthew asked, coming to my side with a worried expression, "Are you alright?"

"No," I told him, "The king…" I couldn't even finish my sentence. It was too awful to say. Genia, however, spoke up.

Chapter 18

The Ruby of Rellene

Princess Anelzea's Point of View

Everyone stared at Genia, horrified. I, however, hadn't heard a word she said. My eyes were glued to a particular ruby, which happened to be on a necklace around Eniela's neck. It took a few seconds for me to be able to form the words.

"Your necklace…" I trailed off.

"My what?" Eniela asked.

"Your necklace: it's vibrating."

Eniela looked down and grinned, clearly relieved.

"I've been waiting for this thing to do something for a long time!" she said with bright eyes.

All of a sudden everything started swirling before my eyes. Feeling dizzy, I stumbled backwards. Eniela was still on the floor, but was soon joined by the rest of us. Then it was all black.

※

When I opened my eyes, I was in a dense, brown forest. A familiar voice asked, "What happened?"

"Verella!" I cried running towards her.

The vider grinned. "Tell me everything."

As I explained what I knew, the rest of the group stood up and walked towards us. Eniela told us about the ruby. "It's the Ruby of Rellene," she told us. "Rellene is an island country which all magical and enchanted things come from," she added, seeing my confused face.

But something in the story still didn't add up.

"Eniela, if your necklace is magic, why haven't you used it before?"

"*Used* it?" she said, amused, "I can't *use* it. It acts on its own accord. It does, however, serve the purposes of the person who wears it. Oh, and it's not magic. It's *enchanted*."

"Oh," I replied simply, not really knowing the difference. Later, Eniela explained to me that enchanted meant someone caused something to have magic, while magical meant that something originally.

"Your Highnesses!" Drandin emerged from the bushes. Verella gave him the what-about-me look that she had to use a lot now. "We need your help," he said, gesturing to something behind the bushes.

I peered through the bushes and gasped. There was an awful battle going on. But the biggest problem was that the Keedans were not just fighting Sydnians. They were also fighting Neivians. My mother pulled a sting arrow from her quiver. She'd lost her arrows and sting arrows were all we had left to give her. She shot the arrow and hit a Sydnian. I was shocked.

"You can…"

She just shrugged with a grin and stunned a few more Sydnians.

※

The battle had barely even started when I lost the bow that Drandin had just given me. I took an arrow from my quiver and swung it wildly, stunning every Neivian that came near me. Before I knew it, I was face to face with Kolla. I brought the hand that held the arrow high above her head.

Her mouth moved but I could not hear her words. When I spoke, I was surprised by my own words: "Your reign will end." My hand dropped and she was stunned.

My heart was pounding. *I just stunned my own aunt*, I thought. I shook the thought off.

She was an enemy.

※

"How did they get there?" I asked after the battle.

"Through the portal. The same one that your parents," someone answered.

Everyone who was not injured stood outside the tent. Not many remarks were made.

The Keedans had suffered a terrible defeat. Most of the people in our group had some kind of injury. Amayda was nursing all the wounded individuals. Suddenly Eniela, who had twisted her ankle and hit her head quite badly, popped her head out of the tent.

"Ashterella! Where is she?"

Chapter 19

Ashterella

Princess Eniela's Point of View

I tried not to wince in pain as we searched for Ashterella. During the battle, Drandin, who had been in a hurry, had given me a crossbow. It didn't take long for me to get used to it, and it was very accurate. The trouble was, it was hard to load the sting arrows.

Drandin later told me that crossbows use bolts, which were like short arrows. Of course, with only a crossbow to protect me, it wasn't long before I was face to face with Fen Wes.

I clutched a sting arrow from my quiver and threw it at him. It hit him, but it didn't penetrate his armor like the others did.

That's when I realized that the Sydnians had made anti-sting arrow armor. I understood why. In Sydnia, being taken prisoner is a great dishonor. No one wanted to risk it.

During my moment of realization, Fen Wes used the flat side of the sword to knock me onto my back. My head hit a rock, causing the world to start swirling. "I'll be back for you later," he whispered menacingly before he carried on fighting.

That was the last thing I could remember.

"Eniela!" a familiar voice called. It was Luka.

His tunic was smeared with dirt, grass, and blood. I wasn't sure where he came from, as he wasn't with the other by the tent.

The medicine Amayda had made from some herbs helped with the pain in my ankle, but it still hurt very much. My friend came to my side, offering a hand to help me balance better.

"Are you alright?" he asked, already knowing I wasn't. I had trouble not bursting into tears at that moment, and a few tears slipped down my cheek. Luka helped me onto the ground to get weight off my ankle.

"Eniela!" Anelzea called loudly from some bushes.

※

Ashterella was lying in the bushes, breathing hard and crying. She had no injuries, thank goodness. "Eniela!" she cried happily when she saw me. I breathed a heavy sigh of relief and I squeezed Luka's hand.

"What happened?" Anelzea asked.

"Trett hid me here," she answered, naming a noble Keedan soldier. Trett was Drandin's younger brother and was a very noble man.

"Oh no!" I cried suddenly, as a thought hit me, "Fen Wes saw the necklace, didn't he?"

"Yes," Anelzea answered, confused.

"He knows there's an enchanted necklace. And he knows I have it."

"And he'll do anything to get it," Anelzea finished for me.

Chapter 20

Myads

Princess Anelzea's Point of View

"But Eniela," said Ashterella, "That necklace can't be taken off." I breathed a sigh of relief, but I was the only one. Everyone was looking at each other, as if everyone was afraid to move.

"Unless…" Luka trailed off.

Eniela finished his sentence, her voice shaking, "Myads."

"Myads?" I asked, "What's a myad?"

"A myad can grant one wish and then she or he dies," Eniela replied, biting her lip.

"None of them would grant a *Sydnian's* wish, though." I pointed out.

"Maybe not an adult, but a child wouldn't know better."

I gasped, "You said that when a myad grants a wish it dies? Fen Wes would do that to a *child*?" I wasn't sure I could believe it. Yes, Fen Wes was awful, but that seemed way too far.

"Fen Wes does terrible things," Luka said in a tone that suggested plenty of experience with the soldier, "He would definitely cheat a child."

Silence followed, until I spoke up, "Maybe they won't think of the myads." I wanted to cross my fingers and hope they wouldn't, but Eniela's next words broke that hope.

"That's the problem," Eniela answered, "They resort to myads whenever they want something."

"They put their own wants in front of someone's life?"

"They're terrible," Matthew muttered darkly.

"We need to stop Fen Wes," said Drandin, "In the meantime, Eniela needs armed guards. Soon all of Sydnia will know that she has the necklace. Only once they try will they find out the necklace cannot come off."

"That means they are coming for *me* and not the myads," Eniela said, her eyes wide with fear, though I knew she was unhappy with the guard idea.

✵

"What I don't understand is how people from all different places got here through the same portal," I said when we got back to the tent. We had sent tayel messages to Lenqua, Schipher, and Keedah telling them to prepare for a battle at Myad Peak, which was one of the highest points of Mount Chaligual.

"When a portal is made without specification of where it goes it can go multiple places." Trett explained, "Getting to them intentionally is possible (that's how we got here and doubtless the Sydnians as well), but I know your parents came on accident. You can't choose where you're going when you go *through* them, though."

"Oh. Maybe we could go through the portal and hope we end up in the somewhere good."

"Considering all of the other places we could end up, that is a really bad idea."

"Never know if you never try," I argued.

I began to walk towards the portal with Amayda following me silently. Trett shrugged and got up, followed by the rest of our group, save Luka, who was writing an account of the battle. (Apparently Schipherians have a record for every single battle involving their country.)

We all stepped in one by one.

Chapter 21

The Castle

Princess Eniela's Point of View

As the mist cleared, I didn't see the palace. In fact, I didn't see Anelzea or anyone else in our group. Remembering my book on portals, I realized that most of the time, people got separated in unspecified portals. Of course, I was the one who had to end up in the capital of Sydnia.

Ironically, it was called Nia. I knew I was in trouble because the royal family lived in Nia, including my sworn enemy Prince Rallash.

Then it hit me, I wasn't just in Nia, I was in the royal portal room. Nia was actually quite near the border of Keedah, but I would never get out of Nia without being recognized, much less the castle.

I suddenly realized, however I was in the portal room. I could go anywhere.

My love my country crept into my mind, saying, "You could find out the Sydnians' plans." As my logical side laughed at the idea, I try to figure out what to do. "I can always get home," I told myself, glancing towards the portal to Keedah. *(Why do they have a portal to Keedah? It would be impossible for a Sydnian to get through the palace without getting caught…)*

But the door is most likely locked, I thought.

I went and tried the door; to my surprise, the door opened. I wanted to spy.

Ignoring my logical side, I stepped into the hallway. It was eerily empty, causing a cold shiver to slip up my spine.

Without a plan, I begin to wonder around the centuries old castle. As I wandered the north end of the castle, I heard an all too familiar voice talking to someone.

It was Fen Wes, no doubt talking to someone of importance. I caught my breath, almost afraid to breathe, as I put my ear on the door.

"Thrinian told me that they were trying to rescue Genia," Fen Wes was saying, "and they brought a vider along."

"Then someone else of that group must have been from Lorrainia," a voice growled. I knew I had heard the voice before, but I could not put a finger on who it belonged to.

"Eniela has the Ruby of Rellene," Fen Wes whispered suddenly.

"We need to get it from her," said the other voice.

"She's a weak little thing. It will be easy."

My face grew red, but I smiled. *I'm not sure that easy is the right word*, I thought.

"Maybe will bait her with one of her sisters. She still has no idea that Genia was just bait."

I couldn't help it, I gasped. Two men fell silent, making me afraid that they heard me. Then the door opened.

Chapter 22

Sanzwahan

Princess Anelzea's Point of View

As I stepped through the portal I was quickly aware that I was alone. As I tried to figure out what to do (and where I was), someone else came through the portal.

"Matthew! Where are we?"

"Sanzwahan, I think," he answered, shielding his eyes from the sun, even though it was setting.

"Is that good?" I said, even though it sounded childish.

Matthew nodded, "Myad Peak is on Sanzwahan."

My eyes bulged. "So we're exactly where we need to be?"

"Well, not *exactly*. We're in the middle of the island, judging by all these trees. The myads are in the north end," he answered.

"Oh. Well, Matthew, lead on."

"Who made a portal in the middle of Sanzwahan?" I heard him mutter.

"By the way," I asked, "is Sanzwahan its own country?"

"No," Matthew answered, almost amused, "it belongs to Keedah."

"Oh. There aren't many countries in Lydria, are there?"

"Thirteen in all," he replied shortly.

"Thirteen?"

"Six big countries take up most of the land. Most of the other countries are islands."

"Oh," I said, "In Lorrainia, there are ten."

"Only ten?"

"Yes," I answered, "But there's also Enchanted Islands. Three of them. One is Dia and it's a little like your Rellene. There's also The Land of Mystery; no one goes there. The Treacherous Pass has a more complicated story. You see," I told him, not caring if I was rambling on, "there was once a time when people went to the Pass and came back with stories of monsters and all sorts of queer things."

"Really?" Matthew murmured.

"But thirty years ago a strange and perhaps power-hungry girl of seventeen went to the pass and never came back. Her name was Shaish. After her many people went, including a man who needed medicine or something for his sick wife. I don't know exactly what was there that couldn't be found elsewhere. He was the only one to come back in all of the thirty years since Shaish had gone. He came back empty handed and when asked what he saw there he wrote this song:

If on The Treacherous Pass you tread

Be wary; you have much to dread

Beasts and monsters; like nothing-

Beasts and monsters you've never seen

If on The Treacherous Pass you tread

Be wary; you have much to dread

And if you see her

Stop for if you meet her

You will never return

If on The Treacherous Pass you tread

Be wary; you have much to dread'"

"That's," Matthew paused, "frightening."

"Well, when his daughter read this she said, 'Is this all you can say?' And this is the strangest part. After she said that he looked at the paper for a moment, screamed, and ran out of the room. No one ever saw him again."

We walked in silence after this, though I heard Matthew humming the eerie song I had sung. I assumed I'd gotten it stuck in his head. I grinned, knowing I had rambled on, but I didn't care.

Night fell, but we kept going. We had to get there before Fen Wes. My feet ached terribly but I ignored it. I walked faster. I was afraid of what might happen if Fen Wes got there first. This was a race and we had to win.

As we walked, I heard a sudden sound.

Matthew groaned. "The Night Beast. They live in the forests of Sanzwahan. Ever wonder why we haven't seen any people? *Nobody* wants to live near the Night Beast. The Sanzwahanians all live near the beach."

"What are we going to do?"

Chapter 23

Saved in the Nick of Time

Princess Eniela's Point of View

Thankfully, by the time the door was completely open, I had managed to squeeze behind it. Through the crack I saw Fen Wes and a young man dressed in a royal tunic. It was Prince Rallash. Or, as I liked to call him, "Prince Radish."

The two men turned and went back into what I assumed was the conference room. Silently sighing a breath of relief, I slipped out of my hiding place and crept down the hallway.

My hopes soared as I saw the portal room. *Whew! That was close*, I thought.

"You!" someone yelled. I whirled around to face Princes Rallash.

His intimidating stature caused me to back up several inches, but I tried to retain my fierce attitude.

"We'll just take that," someone said behind me as fingers yanked on my necklace. The sudden force caused me to begin to cough.

Recovering from the shock, I elbowed whoever it was behind me in the stomach. I twisted round the person and whoever it was let go of my necklace.

Rushing past the person, I realized it was Fen Wes.

Then I remembered some said that secret passages were built throughout the castle.

I didn't try to sneak around this time.

I just ran.

Leading them away from the portal room, I looped back round. The prince was gaining on me.

Just as he reached out to grab my necklace and pull

me back, a hand pulled me into the portal room. As I tried to catch my breath, Luka shut the door with a bang.

I didn't bother (or have the breath for that matter) to ask why he was so late.

The Schipherian prince locked the door and turned to smile at me. Breathing heavily, I thanked him silently. He simply nodded in answer and led me into the Sanzwahanian portal.

The blue mist clouded my vision, and I soon lost sight of the portal room and Luka. The sounds of Rallash and Fen Wes yelling soon faded away.

"To warn the Myads," I murmured, answering my silent question as I waited for the mist to clear.

We had to warn them, no matter what.

It was my fault in the first place.

I came up with the plan.

I had the necklace.

It was my fault, and I had to fix it.

When the blue mist finally made way, we stepped out of the portal onto the sand-dirt mix of the Sanzwahan ground. The sun immediately started sharing its abundance of heat. Thankfully, the sun was setting, so it wasn't as hot as usual.

"It's not your fault, you know," Luka told, as though he had read my mind.

I shook my head, "I came up with the plan that failed. That is what caused all this."

He smiled at me and said, "People have a crazy way of making everything that goes their own fault. This isn't your fault, Eniela."

But it was.

It was my fault.

And I knew it.

I had made this mess.

I didn't care what Luka said, it was my fault.

And I knew it.

Chapter 24

The Night Beast

Princess Anelzea's Point of View

Hiding in a bush is *not* comfortable. But while Matthew searched for a safe way to Myad Peak, that was exactly what I had to do. I was afraid. Afraid for Matthew and afraid for myself.

The Night Beast was out there.

I knew it.

I shifted myself to become more comfortable. The leaves made a loud rustling sound. Almost instantly a tentacle grabbed me from my bush.

The Night Beast was awful.

It had nine legs and nine tentacle-like arms. The legs were arranged like a spiders and the arms sat directly on the legs. It was as black as night and its huge head sat on top of its arms.

A ring of eyes went all around the head. It had a huge grin which displayed its impressive fangs.

I knew I couldn't fight it on my own, but Matthew was too far away to hear if I called him.

I pulled a sting arrow out of my quiver and jabbed it in to the Beast. Nothing happened. I repeated this motion over and over until it was finally stunned.

When I found him I told him all that had happened.

"Wow," he said, "That... Anelzea, no one wins battles against the Night Beast."

"He probably wasn't hungry," I said with a smile.

✖

When the sun rose, I could see the faint outline of a mountain. "Myad Peak," Matthew said.

"We're going to make it in time!" I exclaimed, relieved, "We can save the myads, and the necklace, and Eniela!"

He forced a smile but I could tell he was worried.

We had no idea where Eniela was. Or anyone else for that matter.

Chapter 25

Nightmares

Princess Eniela's Point of View

Luka and I stepped out of the portal to be greeted by silence. The sun had just risen and the heat was shielded by the trees. The remaining darkness made it the perfect time for an attack by the Night Beast, which I had no intentions of meeting. Just the stories and legends told about it were enough to deter me from being even interested in it.

Luka shuddered, giving me a cold feeling inside.

"Where are we?" I asked, expecting to see the beautiful beaches of Sanzwahan.

"Well, the forest is in the middle of Sanzwahan, so I would say we're somewhere near the middle," Luka answered.

He pulled a compass from his tunic pocket and studied it for a second I realized it was one of Drandin's old compasses. Drandin must have given it to him.

"If we're going to get to the myads before the Sydnians do, we have to go north," he said as he slipped the bronze compass back into its place.

"And fast," I added, fingering my necklace that started the problem.

"What's wrong?" I asked Luka, noticing his stiff manner.

"I haven't been to Sanzwahan since..." he trailed off.

Then I remembered that Luka and a few guards had been here not so long ago to find a tough material that would make a good defense wall.

Fen Wes had also heard of this material and had come to get it first. He had evoked the Night Beast and released it on Luka and his guards.

The Night Beast killed his best friend: a guard named Vabin.

And his mother disappeared here a few years back.

This was a place of nightmares for Luka.

"I'm sorry," I murmured, giving him a sympathetic glace, "I know its hard..." *It's hard to lose some one you love so much*. I'd meant to say, but I couldn't get the words out. He knew what I meant.

"Anyway, anyway, anyway," he said, changing the subject. That was a personal joke of ours. *Anyway, anyway, anyway* really meant *I don't like this subject; let's change it*. "We'd better hurry before this island gets too hot."

※

We had been walking for a few hours, and the sun was miserably hot. The pain in my ankle returned, thanks to all the walking.

We were now on the beach and out of the forest, which only let the sun pour down more heat on us. It was several more hours of off and on running and walking before I saw the faint outline of a mountain.

"It's Myad Peak!" I shouted excitedly.

I wanted to break into a run, but the heat and humidity stopped me.

It didn't matter.

Myad Peak could be seen in the distance.

More importantly, Fen Wes couldn't.

Chapter 26

Up the Mountain

Princess Anelzea's Point of View

It was a long, steep way to the top of the mountain. There was no shade, whatsoever. We walked for a long time and I was getting very hot. Too hot. My hands were shaking and my forehead was soaked with sweat. I wasn't going to come back to Sanzwahan for a long time, unless I wanted to get sunburn.

"Matthew," I murmured, sitting down on rock

"Anelzea, are you alright?" he asked.

"She's about to faint," I said, hardly able to think right, "And here she goes."

With that remark, everything went black.

※

When I woke up, I was being dragged up the mountain. Matthew had grabbed my arms and I was bumping up and down.

"Matthew," I growled, "I'm awake!"

"Good," he panted, "Get up and walk."

I forced myself to my feet. The outfit that I had borrowed from Eniela was filthy.

"Matthew, how long have you been dragging me?"

"About an hour," he said, offhandedly.

"An hour?" I exclaimed.

He just nodded.

"Let's go."

We kept going.

We had to get there before Fen Wes.

We had to get to the top before it was too late. The heat was pounding down on me, but I managed to break into a run.

Matthew followed my example.

As I ran a cool wind blew in my face. It felt good in the Sanzwahanian heat. I had many bruises from being dragged but they were the least of my concerns.

"Matthew, if Fen Wes gets there before us... Eniela said that it works for the owner's purpose. What will happen if Fen Wes gets there first?"

"He'll give the necklace to the King of Sydnia and a lot of things will happen in their favor," the prince paused, "Or he might keep for himself and hope it benefits him."

"Eniela told me it hadn't done anything before," I told him, "Why would it do more for the Sydnians?"

"It might not," Matthew admitted, "but we can't take any chances."

"Will it hurt someone?"

"Sort of. It can't hurt people by itself; it was made to do good. But it may open up opportunities. And the Sydnians always take advantage of opportunities. Which means people will be hurt if the Sydnians get the necklace," he paused, "Lots of people."

I ran faster than ever.

I wasn't going to let that happen.

Chapter 27

Sydnians

Princess Eniela's Point of View

It had only been a few minutes since we had first spotted the large mountain, but it seemed like it had been hours. The sun beamed down mercilessly, taking no breaks. I had not been to the north side of Sanzwahan before, as the south side was much cooler.

"Why couldn't Myad Peak be on the south side?" I grumbled.

"Why does Myad Peak have to be on Sanzwahan?" Luka countered.

"Look!" I exclaimed, pointing to two figures in the distance. There were two people making their way up the mountain.

"Who are they?" Luka asked, shielding his eyes from the sun.

"Are they Sydnians?" I squinted. The mountain was a lot closer now, thanks to our fast walking. But now, we broke into a run. I could soon see the figures running as well.

"I would guess," Luka panted. His black hair was ruffled, and lined with sweat.

The heat and humidity were not helping whatsoever.

"Fen Wes?" I murmured, almost afraid to say the name out loud.

"I hope not," Luka said, fingering the sword that hang from his belt.

"Luka," I stopped in my tracks, "I don't think I can do this."

"What do you mean?" he asked, confused at my sudden lack of "bravery".

"I'm *not* brave," I paused, watching his questioning face, "I'm just angry." I decided it was time to tell someone what I was feeling. "Anger has driven everything," I admitted, "If I weren't so angry at them-"

"Eniela," Luka cut me off, "Don't tell yourself that. You are brave, but you just don't see it." Silence filled the air for a moment. "Would anyone not brave-"

"You mean a coward?"

"Yes. Would a, er, coward decide to risk being seen in Sydnia for her sister?"

"Luka, that's different. I-"

"Would a coward have fought in a battle like you did?"

"No," I admitted, with a slight smile. Luka always knew what to say.

"Exactly. Because you are brave."

"Thank you."
He squeezed my hand as we headed off to the mountain.

"Wait a minute!" I exclaimed. "That looks like Anelzea's pouch!"

I then saw the figure reach over her shoulder and finger arrows in a quiver. "It's Anelzea!"

"That looks like Matthew's sword," Luka said.

We took off running like there was no tomorrow. *And there might not be* I thought to myself as we continued running. One more thought slipped into my mind as we sprinted toward the mountain. It was a verse from an old Keedan poem.

Bravery does not always equal victory,

But what brings victory is peace.

Anger only brings misery,

While peace causes enmity to cease.

What will ire bring but battle?

Harmony will only bring hope.

Combat is simply prattle,

While amity brings hope to the globe.

But for peace there must be conflict.

Peace will not come on its own.

You must for peace as long as the evil afflict.

Oh, if fallen empires of the past only could have known.

For concord is fought for, but often itself is lost.

Victory becomes all that matters,

At whatever cost.

Fight only for harmony, for it will not come on its own.

It is when the fight breaks peace, that the true reason is shown.

Was this war about fighting for peace in Lydria? Or what it about power and victory? I couldn't be sure. It didn't matter. Whether it was for revenge, victory, or peace, we had to win that war.

Chapter 28

Myad Peak

Princess Anelzea's Point of View

When we reached the top of the mountain, we were greeted by myads. Their form was the same as a human's but they were slightly taller and had hair the color of the sea. They were so graceful, like an ocean wave. They moved as if water was surrounding them, making their movements flowing and slow.

"Have you come with a wish?" asked a female myad approaching us.

"Not a wish but a warning," Matthew said, "Fen Wes comes this way with a evil wish. He will deceive the children if you don't hide. Go quick as far as you can."

"Matthew!" I shrieked.

Fen Wes and his army were coming up the west side of the mountain. That was one of the two sides that faced the sea.

The color drained from Matthew's face. "Run!" He breathed.

✕

Near the bottom of the mountain, we were met by Luka and Eniela. They were happy to join company again. We knew we had to fight until our armies started to arrive.

As we walked towards the Sydnian army, Amayda, Trett, and Drandin emerged from various spots in the forest. I thought about my parents, hoping they were all right. None of us said anything. Later, I asked Drandin and Trett how they got here, and they told me they ended up in Nievia. They found the portal in the field and went through, ending up in the Keedan palace. From there, they came to Sanzwahan by another portal.

We met the army a small distance from the cove.

The last battle of the Tri-War began right there and then.

※

As we struggled to fight, the armies began to arrive. The first was the Lenquan. As I fought, (I had picked up a bow I had found lying on the scene of the last battle) I saw a launched rock collide with Matthew's head. He collapsed onto the ground.

"Matthew!"

At the sound of the prince's name several Lenquans looked over, worried.

I ran to Matthew, and so did King Ciyang, Matthew's father.

"It's alright," I told the king, "I'll defend him."

The king, who I could tell was still worried, mumbled something like, "I already lost Tasha. I can't lose him." I couldn't make sense of his words.

I pulled out an arrow and put it in my bow. Every time someone tried to attack Matthew and me, they were quickly stunned. The stunned soldiers created a wall around me. Through a gap in the wall of soldiers, I saw a shower of arrows flying towards Eniela. I grabbed Matthew and dragged him to a nearby cave. (Payback for on the mountain) Then I rushed towards Eniela. To my relief she was only stunned. Of course they would have used sting arrows on her. They needed her alive. I picked up my friend and hid her with Matthew.

I looked up at the mountain, and to my horror saw a young myad who had been left behind not too high up. And next to him was Fen Wes.

Chapter 29

Stunning

Princess Eniela's Point of View

I was making good use of my crossbow, and, though I didn't tell Anelzea, I was shooting real bolts, not sting arrows. After all, the Sydnians had invented sting arrow proof armor.

Not to mention sting bolts did not exist.

And I wasn't going to go through the trouble of loading sting arrows to be nice to the Sydnians.

They deserved it.

All of a sudden, arrows started to shower me. They were sting arrows. I looked up and saw that the archers were aiming for me.

And that's when everything went black.

✖

Suddenly, the blackness gave way to a little bit of light.

I looked slowly, as the world was spinning around me. I was next to Matthew in a cave, in the position in which I had been stunned. At first, it looked like he wasn't breathing.

Then I realized he was *barely* breathing.

As the world continued to swirl, I tried to walk. Struggling not to fall, I managed to get to the entrance of the cave. The battle was still going, and we were losing.

The Schipherian army had arrived, and was fighting strong. I waited for the swirling to stop, which only took a few minutes.

Knowing I had no chance of finding my crossbow, I took the small dagger I had hidden in my boot. It was a Lenquan dagger Matthew had given me a few years earlier.

I had hidden in there before we tried to rescue Genia. Wherever she was, I hoped she was alright. I hoped that for Ashterella as well.

Ignoring the funny feeling that had settled in my stomach, I rushed down to the battle.

It was like rushing into a storm. Luka was fighting hard alongside the Schipherian army, and I didn't see Anelzea.

But my mind was full of other thoughts. The Turbotine army had arrived, and was making quite a dent in our numbers.

Fighting hand to hand wasn't as easy as using a bow or crossbow, since I actually was in the middle of the battle. I didn't flinch when I received scrapes or bruises.

It was my fault, and I was going to pay for it.

I wasn't going to let my friends pay for it.

I didn't stop when I received a nasty scrape on my arm.

I didn't stop when the land started swirling again.

It was my fault.

I didn't care what Luka said.

It *was* my fault.

I had the necklace.

I had to figure out a way to destroy it.

I returned to the cave to try. I had to.

Whatever it took.

I wasn't going to let my friends get injured.

Or worse.

Chapter 30

Last Minute

Princess Anelzea's Point of View

I rushed up the mountain, Trett right ahead of me. Thankfully, this was a lower peak of the mountain, so it was not as high as the top. We wouldn't have made it in time.

When we finally got to the myad, he was saying, "Your wish is-"

I couldn't speak. The rushed climb had taken my voice. But Trett spoke up.

"No!" he gasped, "If you do this thousands will be at risk! You, yourself will die!"

"Your wish is denied!" the myad said quickly, his face draining color.

Fen Wes reach for his sword with a, "Well, we-" but at that moment, I plunged a sting arrow into his shoulder where there was no armor.

"You say that *far* too much," I snapped at the stunned figure of Fen Wes. I was tired of "Well, well, well."

Trett and I sprinted down the mountain and I started fighting as hard as I could.

I heard the clashing of swords, the singing of bowstrings, cries of agony, and shouts of victory. And only at that moment when all those sound echoed in my ears did

I truly realize just how terrible war was. After receiving a cut from a stray arrow, I decided I need a few minutes to cool down a bit.

I sat down on edge of the cliff which Verella and I were shooting from. My gaze was on the fighting, but my thoughts were far away. It was true; I never showed much emotion. I had a mask. Even when I was a baby I rarely cried. I rarely laughed. Anelzea meant *invisible mask*. Because those words always defined me. *Invisible mask*.

But, that didn't mean I didn't feel emotion. My heart was grieving, and my muscles were sore. If this battle went on for much longer, I wouldn't have the strength to finish it.

I hoped the fighting would be over.

Soon.

It was a while later when I decided to check on Eniela.

I had already sent a second sting arrow up at Fen Wes hitting him once again where there was no armor.

Another two hours before he would wake up.

When I entered the cave, Eniela was furiously trying to pull her necklace off. Her face was red with anger or heat (I wasn't sure which) and the other jewels of the necklace had a few dents.

She was obviously trying to get rid of it.

"You *know* you can't do that."

She frowned. "I should at least try."

"Why? All you're doing is wasting time. What good will you do trying to fight the charms."

She sighed. "Very well, then."

And before I could say anything, she ran into the battle.

She was determined.

I saw my friend disappear into the fighting with her dagger. I couldn't help but wondering if all of us would survive this battle.

I dearly hoped so.

Chapter 31

A Break in the Battle

Princess Eniela's Point of View

The battle was getting worse and worse as the day wore on. The sun mercilessly poured heat down upon us, with no intentions of cooling down for many hours. My muscles were sore, and my head was aching, but I could stand it.

Truthfully, I was surprised to still be alive.

Using my dagger meant I had to fight hand to hand, and that was much harder.

※

At evening there was finally a lull in the fighting, as each side figured out what to do. Only a few warriors kept fighting.

"Anelzea?" I asked as I pulled her into the tent. "Does anyone know where Genia or Ashterella are?"

"No, I don't," she told me, her eyes filling with worry. "But I'm sure they're just fine." She paused, unsure of what to say next. "I came face to face with Fen Wes."

"What?" I gasped.

"Trett and I saw a young myad with Fen Wes."

"What did you do?"

"He stopped the myad and I stunned Fen Wes," she said as if it had happened a million times.

"You better tell Luka," I told her, remembering his grudge against the Sydnian.

He would want to hear about this. And to be truthful, I was glad to hear this. It served him right to be stunned.

"What about me?" a familiar voice said. Matthew, who had a large bruise on his head, was standing in the entrance to the tent.

"You're alright!" I said happily.

Anelzea disappeared, I guessed to go tell Luka about Fen Wes.

That's when the flap of the tent opened to reveal a little flower.

A tayel message.

"From Princess Genia of Keedah, a human: Don't worry, Eniela. Ashterella and I are here at the palace, safe and sound."

I breathed a sigh of relief, as did the rest of the tent.

"So, what's our next move?" I asked.

"Let's take it from the books," Drandin said, with a glint in his eyes.

Chapter 32

Fen Wes

Princess Anelzea's Point of View

"Luka!" I called, seeing my friend at the edge of the battlefield, "Luka!" The Schipherian prince had his sword in his hand, not in his sheath. His dark brown eyes were on the battlefield, though little action was happening.

"What is it? What happened?" Luka asked, looking quite worried.

Rather than answering, I pointed at the stunned figure of Fen Wes.

"Eniela thought I should tell you."

Luka's brown eyes narrowed. He began to walk towards Fen Wes. It sent a shiver up my spine.

"Luka," I called.

He stopped.

"Maybe you shouldn't kill him," I said, guessing his intentions. "Maybe just take him prisoner. He knows so much about Sydnia. We might be able to get information out of him."

I was rather excited about this idea.

He nodded. "Your right. Even after the war is over, we will need information. I can't let a grudge get in the way of my country."

As he walked to Fen Wes, I thought about what he had said.

After the war is over. I hoped that would be soon.

I suddenly remembered a conversation I had had with Matthew on our way down Myad Peak.

"Mathew, why did the war start?" I had asked.

"Well, Sydnians were doing some awful things. Too awful to say. The Turbotines were no better. Tension kept building and building. Then Hacoloe joined them and it all just-" He paused, looking for the right word, "Burst."

And now Luka had said *after the war is over.*

When would that be?

Chapter 33

A Plan from the Past

Princess Eniela's Point of View

Luka came through the entrance flap of the tent, followed by Anelzea. She gave me a weak smile, but I could not decode its meaning. Turning my attention to more important things, I skimmed over the map of Lydria that was laying on a large rock. Everyone's eyes were glued on Sanzwahan, searching for a way to defeat the enemy.

"As I said, we'll do it by the books," Drandin said, coming close to the map. "If we distract them in the north, Schipher can take the south…"

"And Lenqua can get the east side and push them against the sea!" I finished.

"We're low on numbers," Matthew said.

"A section of our army can break off and help you push them to the sea," Luka suggested.

"You still have good numbers?" I asked.

"Good enough," Luka mumbled, shoving his hands into his pockets. Most of us knew this plan worked, as it had been used *against* us in the War for Keedah, in the biggest (though not final) battle. We lost that battle badly.

"I think that is a great plan," a voice said. It was King Ciyang, who was flanked by two guards. His gaze went from the map to Matthew. I saw that he was very happy to see his son still alive, but he did not make any big gesture to show it.

"The problem is," I said, "if one of the opposing armies surrounds us, we're done for."

"Good point," Drandin agreed, scratching his head.

"Why don't we just go for it," a big man said. It took me a minute to realize it was The Great Warrior. Of course, my sisters and I knew his real name, but we had promised never to share it. He had saved our lives in the Battle for Keedah. He was known for his skill and recklessness, even though he was getting into his mid forties.

"I agree," said Anelzea, who had come to stand next to me.

"What are we waiting for?" Drandin said, "Let's finish this!"

※

Our tactic was working. The opposing armies were being pressed up to the sea.

I had borrowed a bow from a supply stock, and I resorted to using sting arrows again, since Anelzea was right beside me.

We were firing just as quickly as we could load. I wasn't sure if we were even doing any damage, as the battle was fast-paced and blurry.

"When will this war be over?" Anelzea asked with a frown.

"Most likely after this battle," I replied, watching the fierce battle.

"What do you mean?"

"She means that whoever loses this battle loses the war," Mathew explained.

"Are you alright?" Anelzea asked him, suddenly noticing the bruise on his forehead.

"Yeah," Matthew answered, rubbing his forehead.

"Let's go finish this thing," I said, finished with shooting sting arrows. Once again, I drew my dagger and rushed into the battle. But this time, I had two friends beside me. One old and one new.

The roar was deafening. We all fought alongside the Lenquans to help push the enemies to the ocean. Schipher's numbers were still high, and a large group of them had broken off and were helping Lenqua push against the enemies. Among them was Prince James, who was fighting hard.

I couldn't see Luka, but as it was a battle, that was normal. We were getting closer to the ocean, and Sydnian, Turbotian, and Hacoloean ships came into view. They were planning to flee. That was just fine, as long as the battle ended with us winning. It must have gone on for another hour before the enemies were pushes against the ocean.

As they started boarding their ships, I saw Fen Wes.

The stun must have worn off.

We let them flec.

It meant we won.

We won the war, but barely.

"This war *isn't* over," Matthew contradicted, reading my thoughts. "They are still going to look for a way of revenge."

I caught his meaning.

I had thought Keedah was done with the Sydnians, but here we were.

"Oh," was all I could think of.

※

"What now?" I asked, glad to be back in the safety of the palace.

"I don't know," Anelzea admitted.

I was surprised by this answer. Anelzea always knew what to do.

"Are you going back to Nievia?" I dared to ask.

Chapter 34

Official

Princess Anelzea's Point of View

"Go back to Nievia?" I exclaimed, "Eniela, I wouldn't miss your coronation for the world!" I paused. "Any of them!" I certainly was not going to miss my friend's coronation to go back home to my aunt.

She laughed "Thanks, Anelzea."

"Thank *you* for letting me borrow your clothes." I said with a smile, glancing down at a red dress that Eniela loaned me.

We were in the grand parlor, waiting for news.

"Chroni," I said as a thought stuck me, "Why were there only three battles in this war?"

"Three battles?" she laughed grimly, "You mean, three that *you* fought in. I got word of a battle nearly every few days."

I gaped.

I thought about the war. How constant attackers stopped Luka from capturing Fen Wes, how Matthew and I had happened to end up in the right place in the unspecified portal, and how the war had been won by a technique the Sydnians had invented.

"Why-" I began.

All of a sudden Luka burst in with a triumphant smile on his face.

"The surrender is official. We won the war."

We had been waiting for this for a while because Sydnians had a tendency to back out of surrenders and keep wars going, or so Eniela told me.

But it was official.

The war was won.

※

The *Gloria* was the most beautiful ship I had ever seen. It was an Oakwood ship with big white sails decorated with blue dragons.

I felt a breeze in my face as we sailed and thought that the sea was the most beautiful place in galaxy. The ocean foamed lightly behind the ship, which was rocking gently.

It was wonderful, like a dream.

How could I go back to Nievia when Lydria had so much to offer? Even my parents were there. They had arrived at the palace soon after the battle.

And I still had to figure out Amayda.

Why did she trust me so much?

Why didn't she trust Verella?

Why was she in the important prisoner cell?

Where was she from?

Why was she so quiet?

Who *was* she?

Could I stay?

As I thought this, I knew it couldn't happen. I wished it could. I loved Keedah, with its amazing poetry, simple ways, and unique customs. It seemed so peaceful compared to Nievia, where I would be fighting in another war. I didn't want to leave, but a part of me knew I had to.

Chapter 35

Lenquan Legends

Princess Eniela's Point of View

My stomach was in knots and my heart was pounding as the *Gloria* docked in the Lenquan harbor. Though the coronation wouldn't begin for another hour, I was worried. Anelzea, who guessed my feelings, gave me a smile.

Silently, we boarded the small boat that was to go to shore. It wasn't until we were alone, waiting in the library, that we talked.

"Are you alright?" she asked, her eyes showing her worry.

"No," I told her truthfully, "I don't want to be a crown princess. I don't want to become like Chroni and Corinthia."

"I understand. I know you can't see it," she said, "but I have a problem as well. When I met Kolla during the battle, I told her that her reign would end. Now, I've started this I have to finish it. There will be war in Nievia."

I looked at her face. No fear. No pain. No confusion. Yet, I knew she felt these things. While I watched her, I began to feel a tiny bit jealous. Yes, she had started a war with her aunt, but she was acting like war was still a new thing for her. She had started that war herself. Then I realized that she didn't know the full meaning of war.

She didn't know.

She didn't fully comprehend.

The Keedan War had opened my eyes to the evilness that hung above everyone. Sydnians had killed my parents, drove my sisters and I out of our own country, burned the once beautiful island of Rellene to ashes, and almost kept us from allying with Schipher. Now, in the Tri-War, I understood more. I was out of the dark shadows and could see Lydria in plain light. I wasn't sure if I was afraid, angered, or confused after the war, but I knew one thing: *I knew what war was like.* I knew what the consequences were.

Anelzea acted like she had a worse life, but I wasn't so sure. She had parents to be there for her and talk to her, she had a country which was not constantly being threatened, and she had a life in which she could be herself all of the time,

"Are you alright?" Matthew asked coming through the door.

"Not really."

Anelzea left without a word, guessing I wanted some alone time. I turned my attention to all of the books.

"Wow. We don't have all these books of legends in our palace library," I told Matthew, smiling as I traced the edges of the fragile spines.

"Lenqua is big on legends," he answered, running his hand over a rather large book that sat on a table.

"The Legend of Princess Tasha," I read off of the book. Matthew's eyes shot up from the book he was looking at, surprised. The delicate words engraved into the leather caught my interest. "It's papyrus," I murmured as my hand felt the pages. Papyrus was a sturdy material that was often used in books that were meant to last for many years.

"A lot of the Lenquan books are on papyrus," Matthew told me, grinning broadly.

Carefully, I flipped the cover over. The first page had no words, but a drawing. It was a king and queen standing along the bank of a river. In her arms, the queen held a baby. On the other side, another king and queen stood. The queen was holding her arms out, as if to ask for the baby. Moonlight reflected off of the river and revealed the queen's tears. She was the one holding the baby.

"Wow," was all I could say. The drawing was so striking it made my eyes water. "It's so…"

"Beautiful," Matthew finished. He had come to my side, gazing at the drawing with me.

I flipped the drawing over carefully. On the next page the legend began. I was intrigued. Quietly, we both read the first few pages of the book. It seemed like a very recent story. It told the story of the King and Queen on Lenqua. The queen was pregnant with her second child, but threats arose from Turbotia. When the baby was finally born, the threats became more and more.

"What happens?" I asked Matthew.

"Well," he said, "The King and Queen decided to give the baby girl to a royal family of another country until the war and threats passed. Just when they did, the other country fell into war, and it was too risky to try to get the child back."

"Oh no," I said.

"Then that child was needed in that country."

"The one that she was from?"

"No, the other one. So her parents didn't take her back."

135

"That's so sad," I said. Then something hit me. "Wait, if this is a legend, there's some truth to it."

"Yes," Matthew answered shortly.

"What was the other country?" I asked.

"Well, in this story, it's Keedah."

"Are you saying one of my sisters...?" I questioned, surprised.

"Not at all," Matthew said to cool me.

"Then what?"

"It's you."

"What?" I exclaimed in a whisper, taking a step back.

"You're Princess Tasha." I looked into Matthew's eyes, and I could tell he wasn't joking.

"No," I retorted, "No, I'm not,"

"Yes, you are," he countered, his bright blue eyes looking straight into mine.

"If I'm Tasha then why have I never been told?" I asked him, half expecting him to say he was joking. But he didn't.

"The King and Queen of Keedah never got to tell you."

"Wouldn't Chroni remember?"

"No. You arrived on the day Genia was born. Chroni always thought that you were twins. Everyone did. Don't try to deny it. You're Princess Tasha."

"No, I'm not," I repeated. "I..."

"You're my younger sister," he said. "You're always asking me why I'm so protective of you, and that's the answer."

"How come you never told me?"

"I had to protect you."

"But-" I went to argue, but I didn't have anything *to* argue.

I was speechless.

He explained everything I had missed of my own life and left me alone in stunned silence.

※

My whole world had changed. I wasn't Keedan at all; I was Lenquan. That explained why all my sisters had dark brown eyes and I had bright blue eyes.

The doors opened, and I stiffly and slowly walked up the middle of the room. My blue and silver dressed swished around me, reminding me of the shopkeeper back in the village, before this whole adventure began. Chroni and Corinthia waited at the middle of the room on the platform.

I spotted Anelzea standing nearby, giving me a bright smile.

But it only dimmed my moods.

Something about all this happiness made me feel angry.

How could someone keep this from me?

Everything I knew was a lie!

"Do you promise to govern the people of Keedah with justice and mercy? Do you promise to sacrifice for your people, no matter what the cost?" Chroni asked as I stayed in a deep curtsey, which hurt quite a bit.

"I do promise."

"It is my joy to announce you Crown Princess Eniela of Keedah!" she said loudly. *Of Keedah*. But I wasn't Keedan. I was Lenquan. Matthew's gaze caught mine, and I stared at my brother.

※

"What do you mean stay in Lenqua?" I asked.

"I mean that you could stay here in Lenqua," Matthew said.

"But I've just been announced Crown Princess Eniela of Keedah," I told him, as if he didn't already know that.

"It's your choice, Eniela."

"You expect me to choose?"

"Take your time," he said kindly.

Could I go to live with my *real* family?

Could I live a life with parents?

Could I abandon my "sisters" in Keedah?

What about Ashterella?

I didn't want to leave her. Yet... My heart tied into a knot, leaving me speechless.

Chapter 36

Maybe

Princess Anelzea's Point of View

"Anelzea?" Eniela asked timidly after the feast, "Can I talk to you," she paused, "alone?" I was confused, as I hadn't seen my friend timid before. I nodded and she drew me into a room which probably hadn't been used for years. It had moth eaten arm chairs and small wooden tables with faded floral designs.

We sat down.

Eniela told me about a legend about a Lenquan princess named Tasha, which was very depressing. I couldn't help but thinking why she was telling me this.

"Matthew said that *I* was Tasha," she paused, watching me for my reaction, "And I believe him. He said that his whole family knew. Which makes sense. They always treated me like a daughter. I guess… I guess I am their daughter."

I was speechless for a few moments before I remembered something. "Eniela, when Matthew got hurt in the battle, Ciyang muttered, 'I already lost Tasha, I can't lose him.' But if he knew you were Tasha like you said, why did he say that?"

"Matthew said that my being so far away was hard for his- no, our- father. He felt like he lost me."

I nodded.

That made sense.

"Anelzea, Matthew said I could live here in Lenqua. I just- should I?"

"No one can make that choice but you. I am not one to influence you."

I stood up.

"Wait," she said, "Should I tell my- um- sisters?"

"Yes," I replied with out a delay, "You owe it to them. They need to know."

"I just don't want our bonds to break," she told me.

"They deserve to know."

She nodded. We stood up and hugged. I wasn't sure I was going to see Eniela again, but I knew there would always be a portal. After the victory, I felt as though we could take on the world. She was there to help me. Of course, my face showed none of this, but Eniela's did.

Right outside the door were my parents and Verella.

"It's time," Mother said gently, "We have to go."

I turned to my friend and gave her a hug.

Then without a word, we began our walk to the portal room. Thoughts of this adventure flooded my mind.

As we walked to the portal room, I heard footsteps behind us. I turned around.
"Matthew? What's wrong?"
"Eniela," he replied, looking at his feet, "I'm guessing she has already told you."
I nodded. "Then, what's the problem?"

"I'm afraid she'll pick Keedah. It's all the necklace. Its purpose is to give her a Keedan manner. The Keedan queen and king gave it to her so she wouldn't suspect anything. They didn't want her to find out until the proper time."

"But Matthew, she's Lenquan by birth, not by any enchantment. Her true self has to overpower the enchantments," I told him.

He smiled weakly. "Maybe."

But that "maybe" didn't just mean that maybe she'd stay in Lenqua. It was his way of saying good-bye. He was saying:

"Maybe I will someday repay you for saving my life."

"Maybe you'll forgive me for not trusting you."

"Maybe you can comfort Eniela while I am forced to sit by and watch."

All of this was said in one simple word. *Maybe*.

When we reached the portal, I hesitated, then stepped in. emerging at the top of DeNell's perch. I looked around at the serene surroundings, knowing that it would not be peaceful for long.

Just as the Tri-War of Lydria had drawn to an end, a new war started. The Neivian war.

Pronunciation Guide
And Maps

Amayda *(uh-may-duh)* – *a young girl who spent many years inside of the Sydnians' important prisoners cell; good at medicine and using herbs*

Andromeda *(an-drom-uh-duh)* – *the galaxy which houses the planets of Lydria, Lorrainia, and Teta*

Anelzea *(uh-nel-zee-uh)* – *eldest and only princess of Nievia who is brave and smart; daughter of King Mezule and Queen Pearla; full name of "Anelzea" Fysozzi Keina Stonritra*

Ashterella *(ash-ter-rel-uh)* – *youngest princess of Keedah who looks up to Eniela; daughter of King Meyon and Queen Nereve; full name of Serelle Kah "Ashterella" Deforiad Werellid Rel Kerene*

Brookston *(bruhk-stun)* – *a large city in Keedah which is a primary target of the Sydnians; a city in which Keedans store emergency supplies*

Chroni *(kron-ee)* – *eldest princess of Keedah who is strict and stern; daughter of King Meyon and Queen Nereve; full name of Chronila "Chroni" Dazrell Lort Cuyewl Kerene*

Corinthia *(cor-inth-ee-uh)* – *second princess of Keedah who is shy; daughter of King Meyon and Queen Nereve; full name of Selliene "Corinthia" Aleh Terell Querey Kerene*

Drandin Torin *(dran-din)* – *captain of the Keedan army who is around the palace a lot; brother of Thrinian and Trett*

Eniela *(en-ee-el-uh)* – *third princess of Keedah who is sarcastic and impulsive; "daughter" of King Meyon and Queen Nereve; full name of Greneh "Eniela" Renellea Hilrelin Kerene; Lenquan name of Zallah Tashli ah "Tasha" Sashah Ansley Derl*

Fen Wes *(fen wes)* – *Sydnian general; sworn enemy of Luka and the Keedan princesses; full name of Denrene Quij Fallopeh Roun Fen Degehi Adcul Wes "Fen Wes" Dren*

Genia *(jen-yuh)* – *fourth princess of Keedah who is talented at making things; daughter of King Meyon and Queen Nereve; Genheydehia "Genia" Dalre Faw Aneh Sallemonel Kerene*

Hacoloe *(hac-oh-loh)* – *island country in Lydria; enemy of Schipher; not very populated; peaceful; Schipherian (Tipish) is main language*

James *(jay-ms)* – *eldest prince of Schipher; son of King Regene and Queen Nella; brother of Luka; full name of Vichole Wer Jaemes "James" Rallond Zes*

Keedah *(kee-duh)* – *country in Lydria; enemy of Sydnia; well populated; peaceful; Keedan (Nelicee) is main language*

Knock *(noc)* – *country in Lorrainia; known for long-lasting alliance with Tip; well populated; ready for a fight; Knockesh (Sydnian) is main language*

Kolla *(col-uh)* - *evil queen of Nievia; Anelzea's aunt; full name Rosefy Kolla Stonritra and Emelieah*

Kurah *(kew-raw)* – *a city which was destroyed by the Sydnians in the War of Keedah; a city of ruins*

Lenqua *(lenk-wah)* – country in Lydria; enemy of Turbotia; heavily populated; peaceful; Lenquan (Neivian) is main language

Lorrainia *(lor-uh-an-i-uh)* – world which is claimed by forty countries; main countries are Nievia, Teaf, Knock, Tip, Nellic, and the Seekian Isles

Luka *(lewk-uh)* – second and youngest prince of Schipher who is a very good fighter and is a master of sarcasm; son of King Regene and Queen Nella; brother of James; full name of Dehrrel Nicholas "Luka" Weophuy Zes

Lydria *(lid-dree-uh)* – world which is claimed by thirteen countries; main countries are Keedah, Lenqua, Sydnia, Schipher, Hacoloe, and Turbotia

Matthew *(math-yew)* – eldest and only prince of Lenqua who is caring and a talented swordsman; son of King Ciyang and Queen Zerekka; full name of Faweh Shac Teh Matthe "Matthew" Axel Wen Derl

Menikat *(menee-cot)* – a sour fruit of Keedah

Mezule *(mez-yew-l)* – brother of Kolla; rightful Neivian king; father of Anelzea and husband of Pearla; full name Mezule Kyhem Stonritra

Chaligual *(cha-ling-gwle)* – the largest mountain on the Keedan island of Sanzwahan; houses Myad Peak

Myad *(mie-ad)* – after he or she grants a wish, he or she dies; tall with hair the color of the sea; all live on Myad Peak

Nellic *(nel-lic) – country in Lorrainia; well populated; neutral in war; Nelicee (Keedan) is main language*

Nievia *(nee-vee-uh) – country in Lorrainia; fought against Keedah and their allies in the Tri-War; well populated; peaceful; Neivian (Lenquan) is main language*

Pearla *(perl-uh) – rightful Neivian queen; mother of Anelzea and wife of Mezule; full name Riadom Pearla Jofira Vawlyn Stonritra*

Rellene *(rel-ee-ne) – magical island country in Lydria; mostly destroyed by Sydnia; not very populated; peaceful; old Lenquan is main language*

Sanzwahan *(sawnz-wuh-hon) – a small island of Keedan in the Great Ocean; known for being very hot; home of the Night Beast*

Senwerei *(sen-ware-ee) – sixth princess of Keedah who is inwardly friendly but a little shy; daughter of King Meyon and Queen Nereve; full name of Zehrenah Trachi "Senwerei" Jahil Kerene*

Seekian Isles *(seec-ee-en i-ls) – country in Lorrainia; the royal family is a relation of Anelzea; well populated;*

Silche *(silch-ey) – young errand girl from the village*

Schipher *(sie-fer) – country in Lydria; enemy of Hacoloe; heavily populated; ready for a fight; Schipherian (Tipish) is main language*

Sydnia *(sid-nee-uh) – country in Lydria; enemy of Keedah; crowded country; ready for a fight; Sydnian (Teafish) is main language*

Turbotia *(ter-bo-tee-uh) – country in Lydria which is originally a Sydnian settlement; enemy of Lenqua; well populated; ready for a fight; Sydnian (Teafish) is main language*

Teaf *(teef) – island country in Lorrainia; well known for sailing; heavily populated; ready for a fight; Teafic (Sydnian) is main language*

Tip *(tip) – country in Lorrainia; known for the long-lasting alliance with Knock; well populated; neutral in war; Tipish (Schipherian) is main language*

Thrinian Torin *(thrin-ee-en) – captain of the Keedan archers who taught Eniela to use a bow; brother of Drandin and Trett*

Trett Torin *(tret)- a noble soldier of Keedah; brother of Drandin and Thrinian*

Verella Evadell *(ver-el-uh) – vider of Nievia; friend of Anelzea who is a talented archer; descendant of the vider who found Nievia*

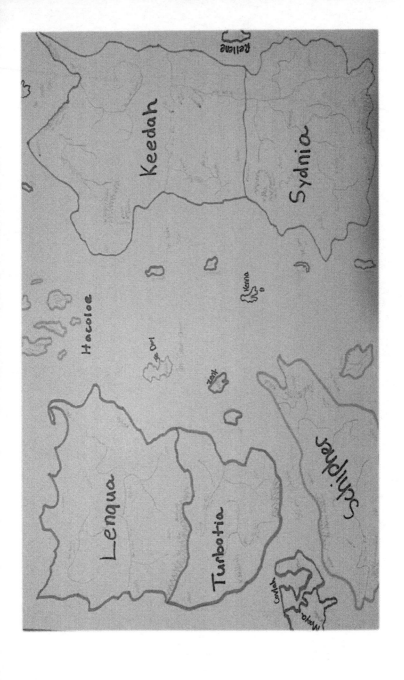

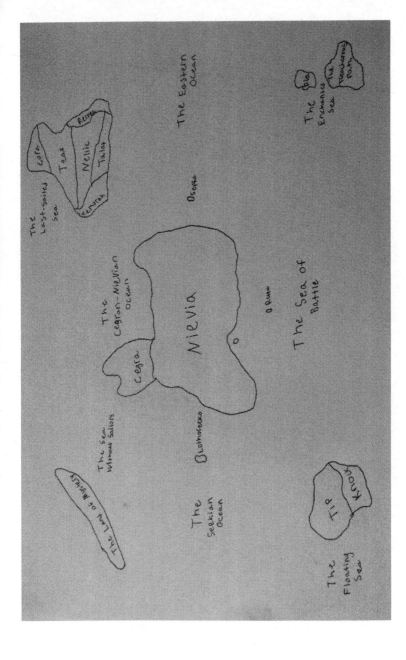

ABOUT THE AUTHORS

Annabella Lorraine Bouk is a quirky teenage author and bookworm. She loves adventure novels, which she feels can take the reader on a journey. She enjoys singing, acting, and learning pointless facts, but in the end she loves to curl up with a book and a cup of tea. She can't wait to write more of the series with her close friend and fellow author.

Pamela Brooke McIlrath is a thirteen-year-old writer and a music lover. When she is not writing or reading, Pamela likes to sing, dance, act, and writing poetry. "I'm really happy," Pamela says, "to finally share the thrilling tales of the Andromeda Galaxy with the world. Of course, it couldn't have been possible without my fellow author Annabella, who has made this endeavour a lot more fun."

"Bravery does not always equal victory,
But what brings true victory is peace.
Anger only brings misery,
While peace causes enmity to cease.
What will ire bring but battle?
Harmony will only bring hope.
Combat is simply prattle,
While amity brings hope to the globe.
But for peace there must be conflict.
Peace will not come on its own.
You must fight for peace for as long as the evil afflict.
Oh, if fallen empires of the past only could have known.
For concord is fought for, but often itself is lost.
Victory becomes all that matters,
At whatever cost."

- From 'The Fight for Peace' (a Lydrian Poem)